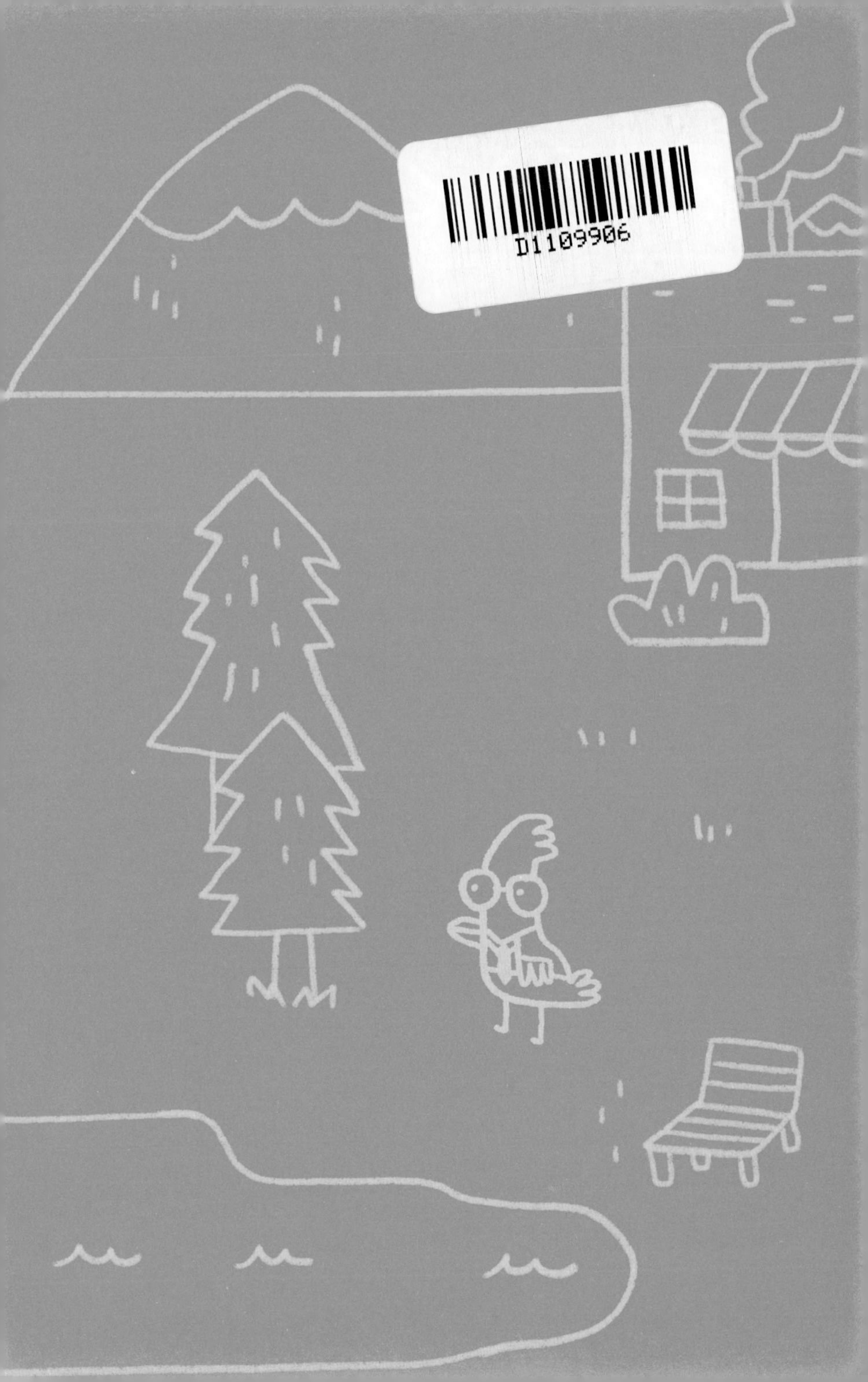

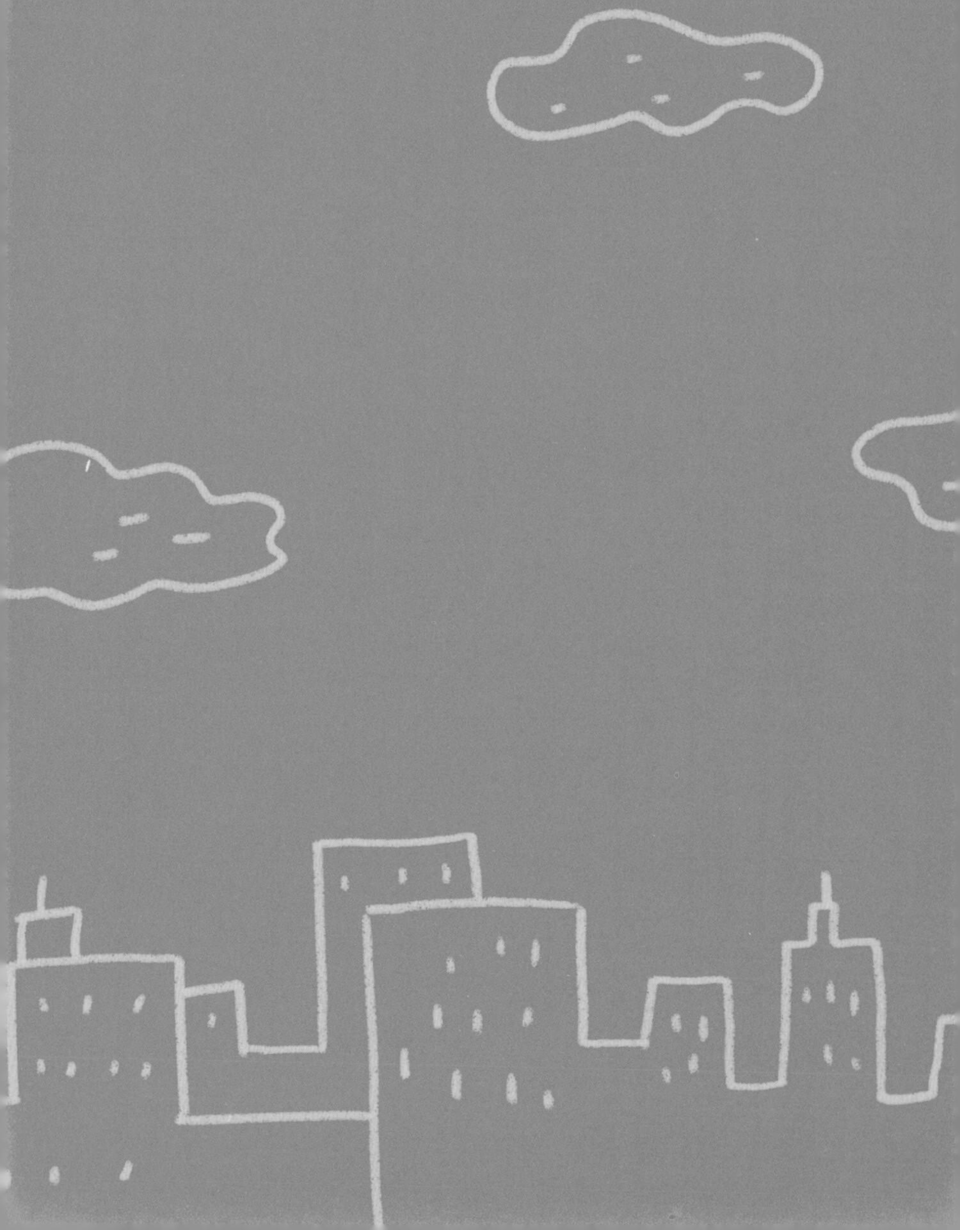

DOODLE ADVENTURES®

THE RISE OF THE

RUSTY

ROBO-CAT!

THE RISE OF THE

RUSTY

ROBO-CAT!

MIKE LOWERY

WORKMAN PUBLISHING
NEW YORK

Library of Congress Cataloging-in-Publication Data is available.

ISBN 978-0-7611-8721-9

Workman books are available at special discounts when purchased in bulk for premiums and sales promotions as well as for fund-raising or educational use. Special editions or book excerpts can also be created to specification. For details, contact the Special Sales Director at the address below, or send an email to specialmarkets@workman.com.

Workman Publishing Co., Inc.
225 Varick Street
New York, NY 10014-4381
workman.com

WORKMAN and DOODLE ADVENTURES are registered trademarks of Workman Publishing Co., Inc.

Printed in China
First printing May 2017

10 9 8 7 6 5 4 3 2 1

DEDICATED TO THE TWO
BEST HUMANS ON EARTH:

→ KATRIN AND ALLISTER

HELLO,
JUNIOR AGENT.
WELCOME TO THE
DOODLE ADVENTURE
SOCIETY'S MISSION CENTER.

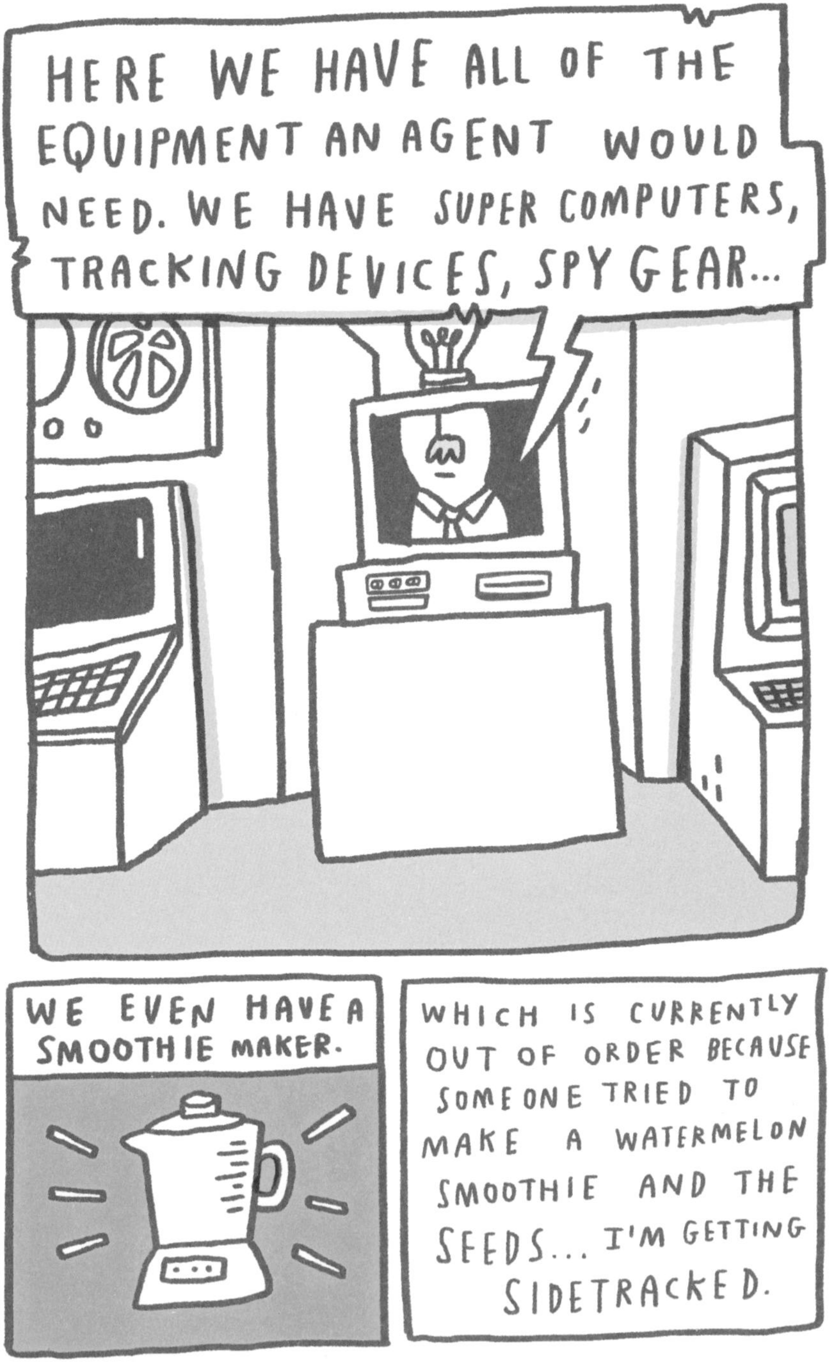
HERE WE HAVE ALL OF THE EQUIPMENT AN AGENT WOULD NEED. WE HAVE SUPER COMPUTERS, TRACKING DEVICES, SPY GEAR...
WE EVEN HAVE A SMOOTHIE MAKER.
WHICH IS CURRENTLY OUT OF ORDER BECAUSE SOMEONE TRIED TO MAKE A WATERMELON SMOOTHIE AND THE SEEDS... I'M GETTING SIDETRACKED.

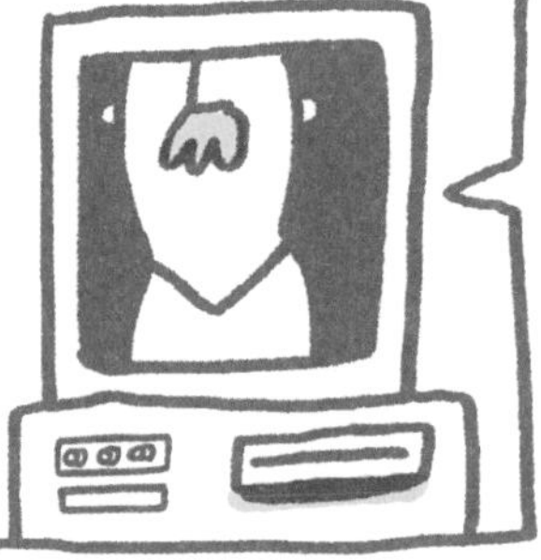

WE CALLED YOU HERE BECAUSE WE HAVE AN IMPORTANT MISSION FOR YOU. WE'VE ASKED AGENT 86B37

TO BE YOUR GUIDE, BUT HE IS RUNNING LATE FOR SOME REASON.

WHILE WE WAIT WE CAN GET YOU

WARMED UP.

THIS MISSION IS GOING to REQUIRE A **LOT** OF DRAWING, SO LET'S SEE IF YOU'VE GOT WHAT IT TAKES!

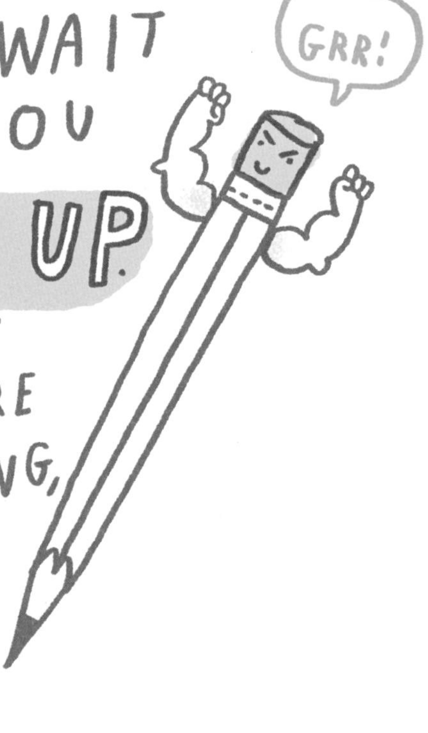
GRR!

LET'S START SORT OF
EASY. CAN YOU DRAW A

SPACE

VAMPIRE ?

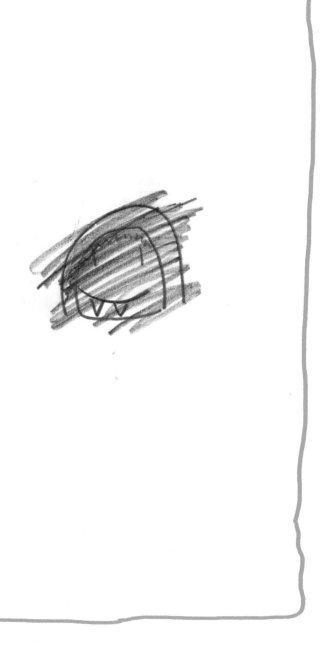

THAT WAS GREAT. LET'S TRY SOMETHING A LITTLE HARDER. CAN YOU DRAW A MONSTER EATING ITS FAVORITE FOOD?

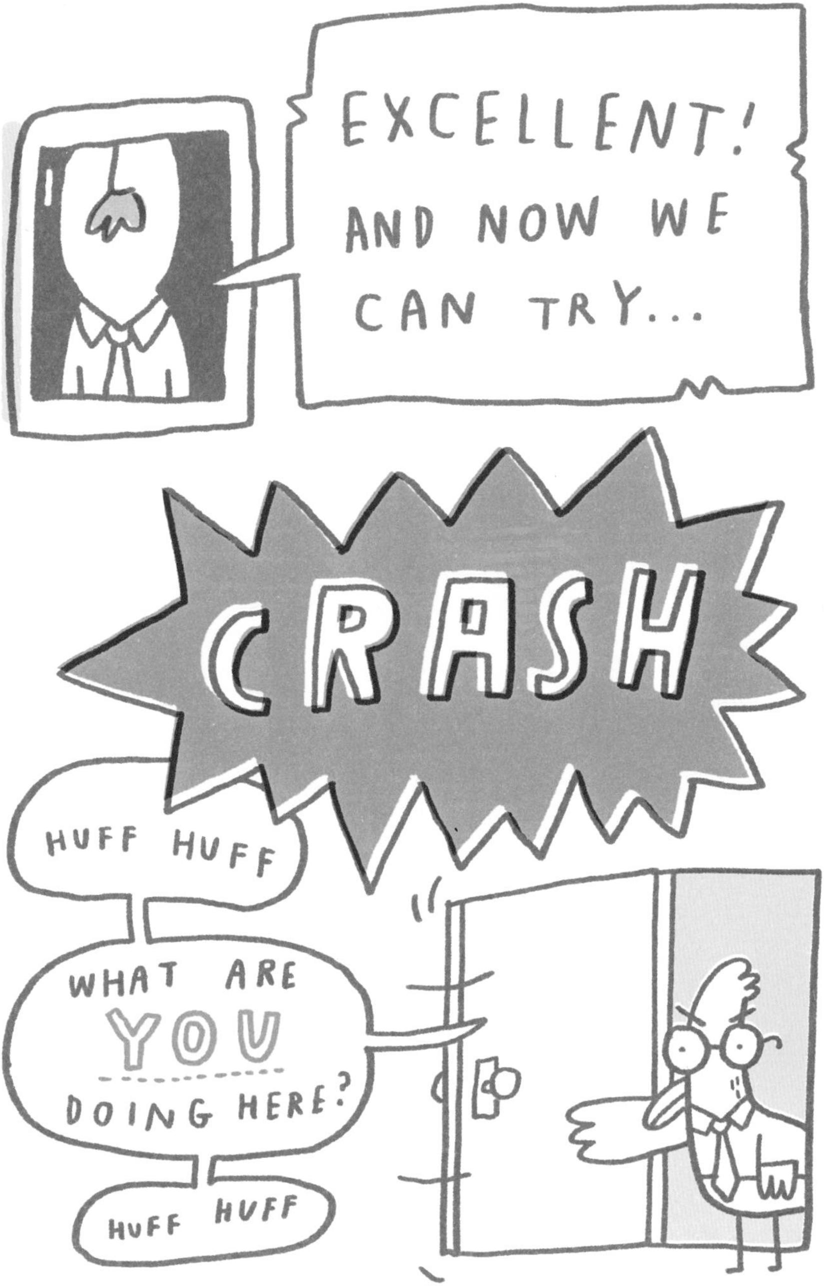
EXCELLENT! AND NOW WE CAN TRY...
CRASH
HUFF HUFF
WHAT ARE YOU DOING HERE?
HUFF HUFF

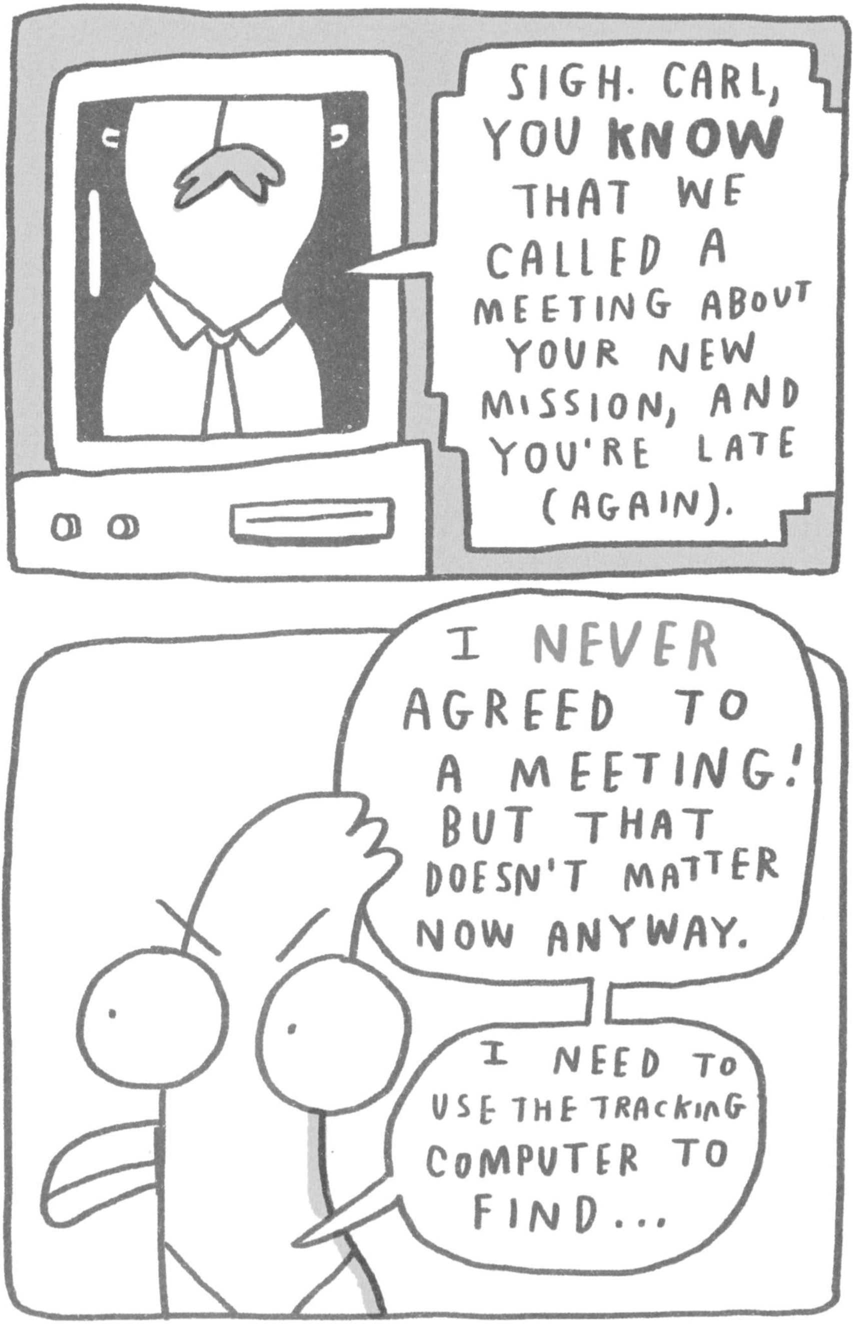
SIGH. CARL, YOU KNOW THAT WE CALLED A MEETING ABOUT YOUR NEW MISSION, AND YOU'RE LATE (AGAIN).
I NEVER AGREED TO A MEETING! BUT THAT DOESN'T MATTER NOW ANYWAY.
I NEED TO USE THE TRACKING COMPUTER TO FIND...

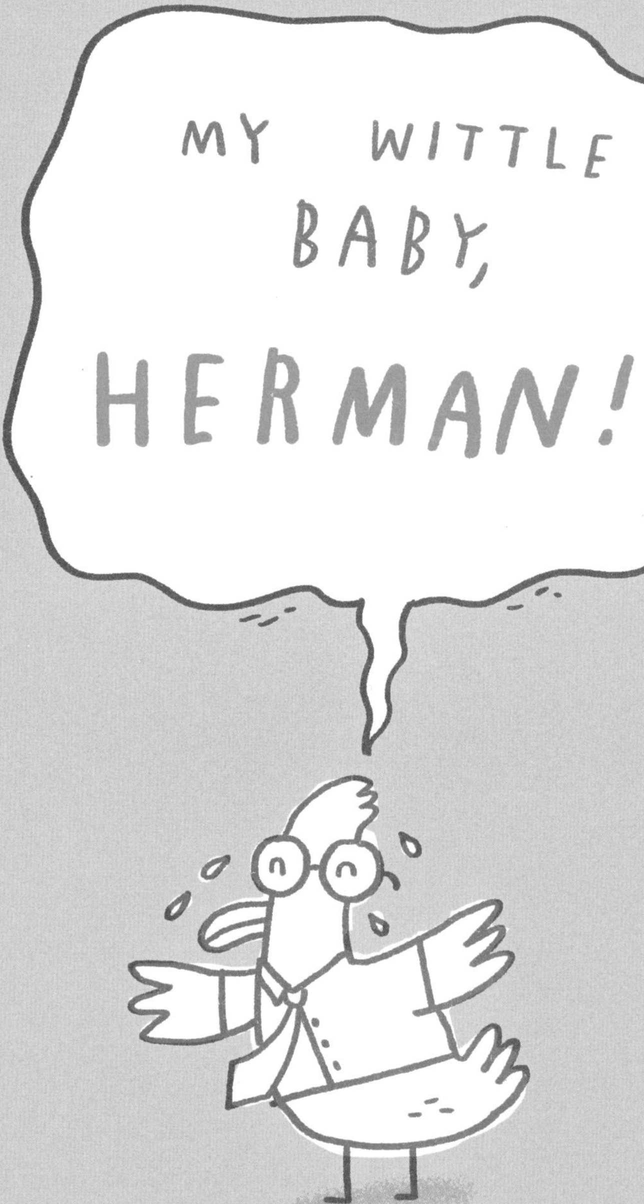
MY WITTLE BABY, HERMAN!

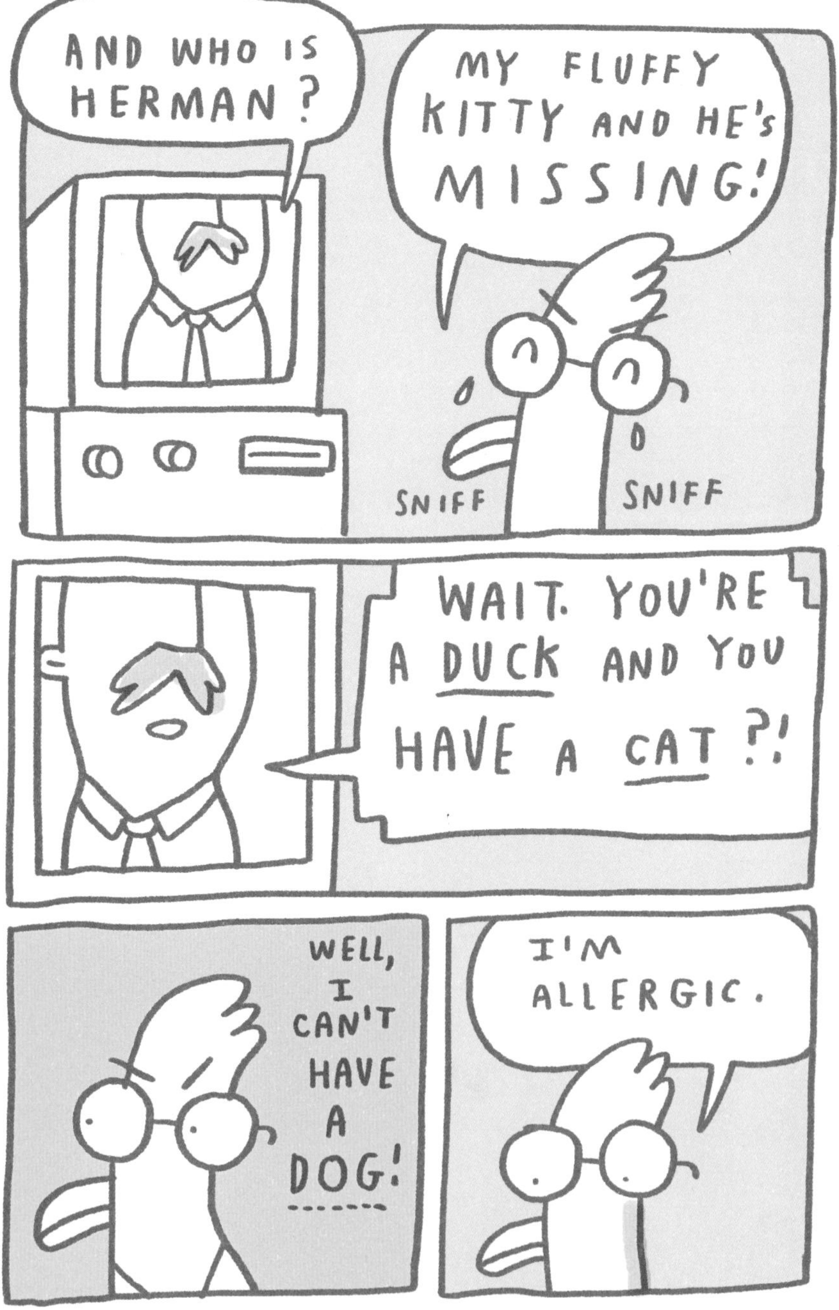
AND WHO IS HERMAN?
MY FLUFFY KITTY AND HE'S MISSING!
SNIFF
SNIFF
WAIT. YOU'RE A DUCK AND YOU HAVE A CAT?!
WELL, I CAN'T HAVE A DOG!
I'M ALLERGIC.

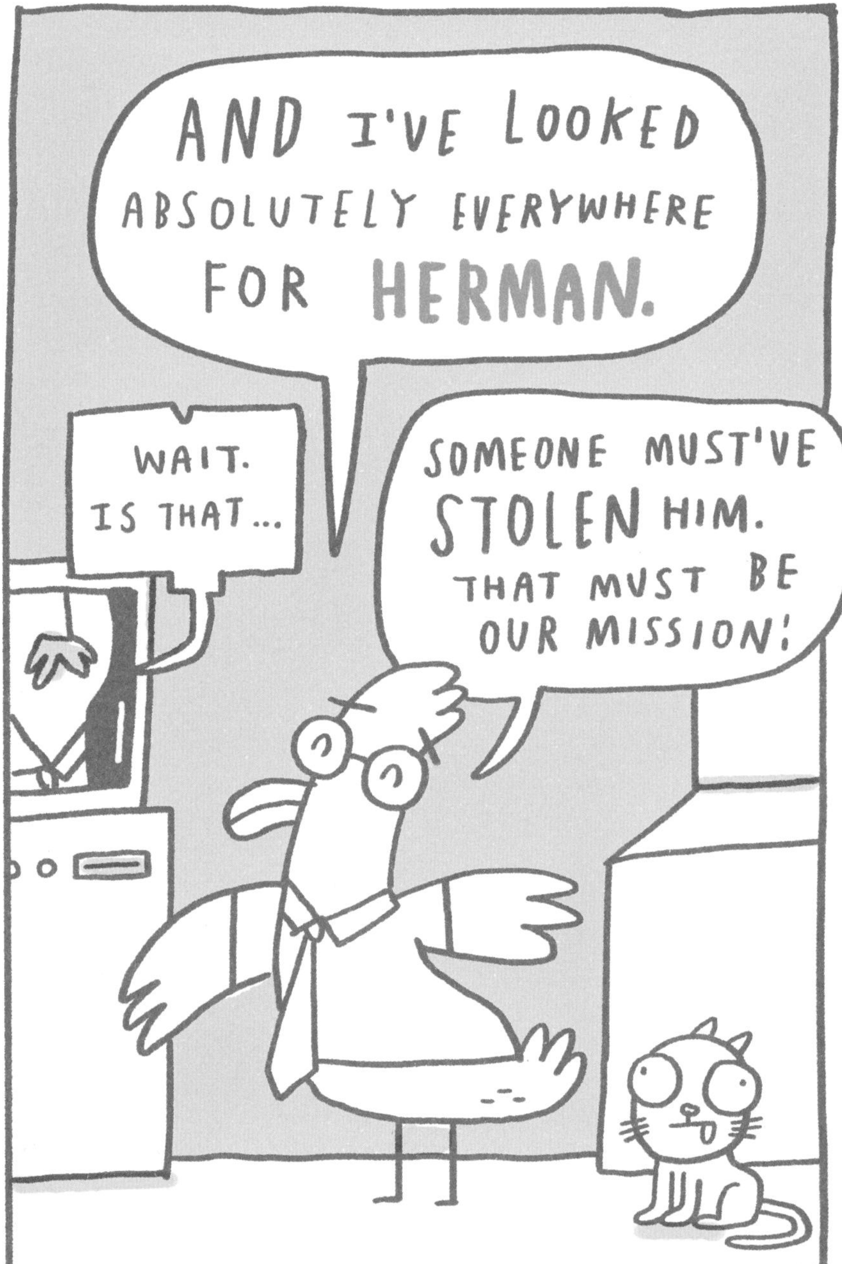
AND I'VE LOOKED ABSOLUTELY EVERYWHERE FOR HERMAN.
WAIT. IS THAT...
SOMEONE MUST'VE STOLEN HIM. THAT MUST BE OUR MISSION!

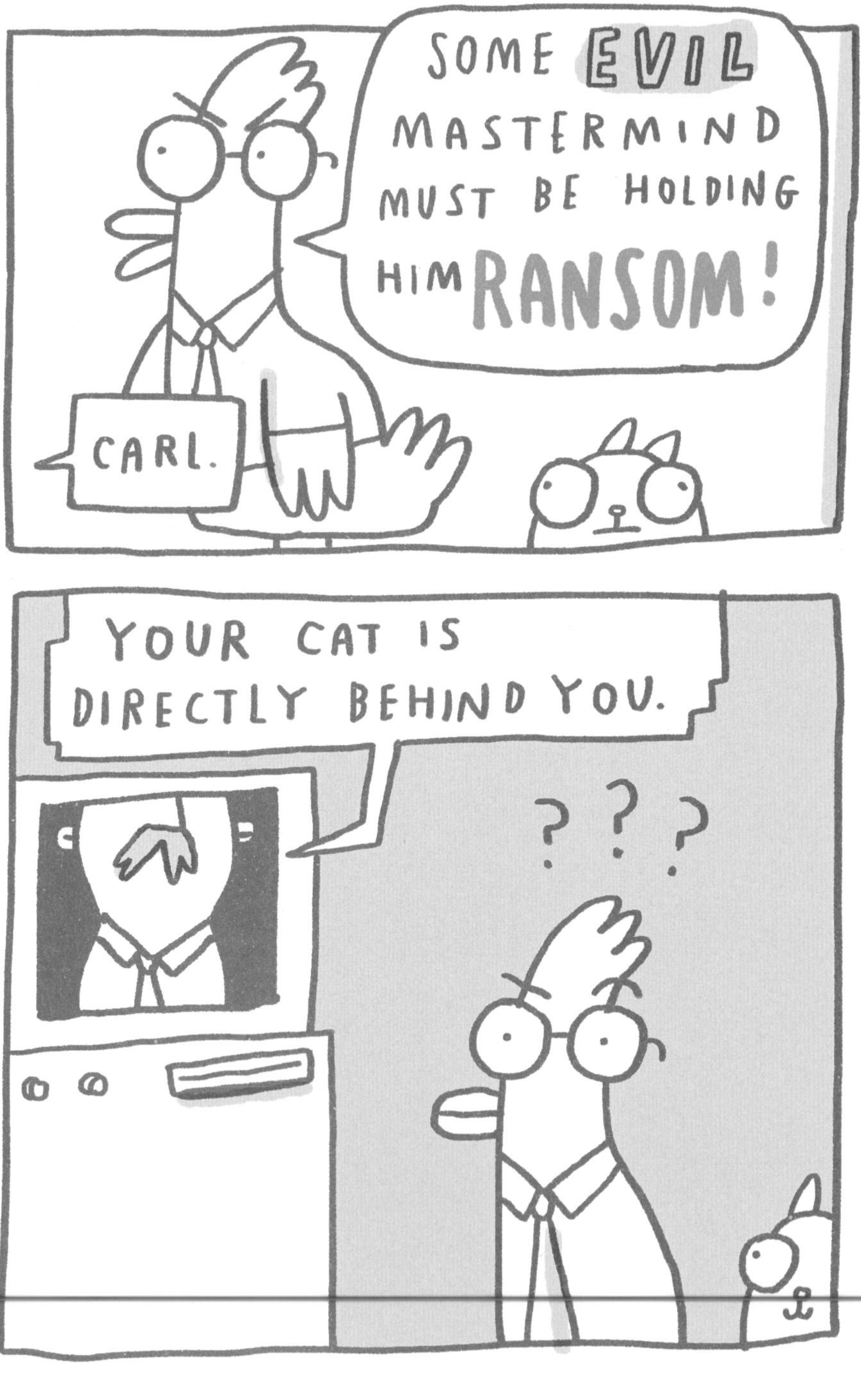
SOME EVIL MASTERMIND MUST BE HOLDING HIM RANSOM!
CARL.
YOUR CAT IS DIRECTLY BEHIND YOU.
???

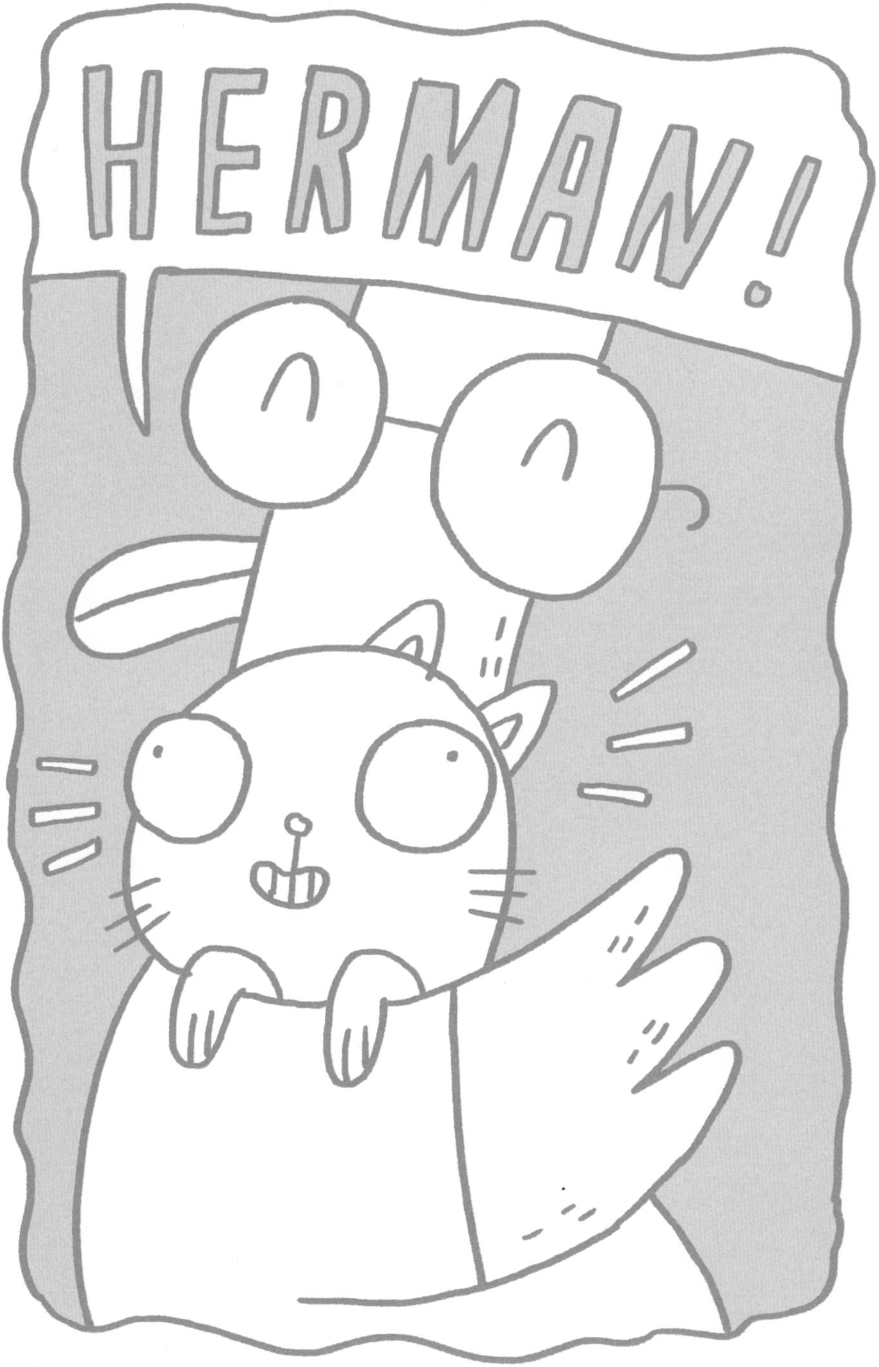
HERMAN!

I FOUND YOU ALL BY MYSELF.

YOU HAVEN'T EATEN IN THIRTY MINUTES. YOU MUST BE STARVING!

DRAW A SNACK FOR HERMAN.

 UH-OH. HE DOESN'T SEEM TO LIKE THAT. TRY AGAIN . MAYBE DRAW SOME SWEETS!

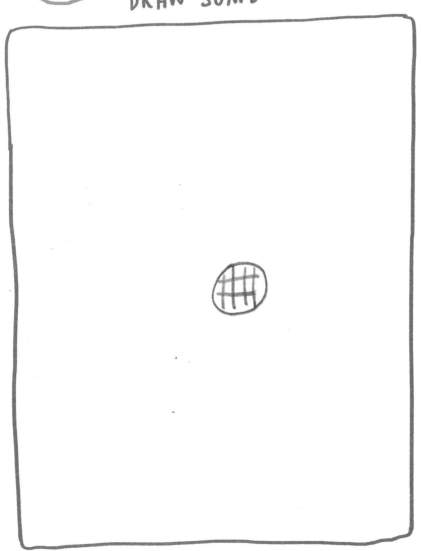

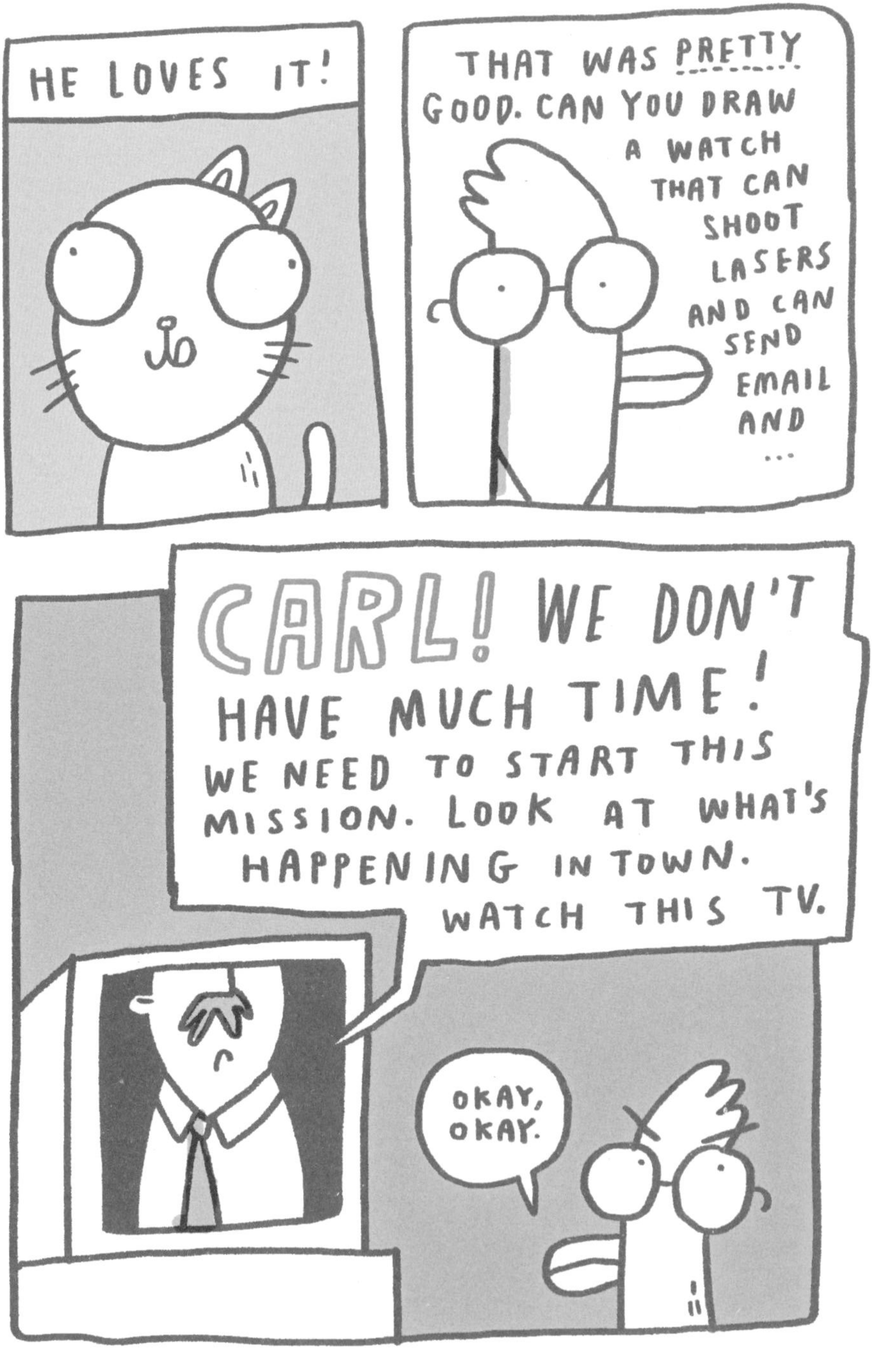
HE LOVES IT!
THAT WAS PRETTY GOOD. CAN YOU DRAW A WATCH THAT CAN SHOOT LASERS AND CAN SEND EMAIL AND ...
CARL! WE DON'T HAVE MUCH TIME! WE NEED TO START THIS MISSION. LOOK AT WHAT'S HAPPENING IN TOWN. WATCH THIS TV.
OKAY, OKAY.

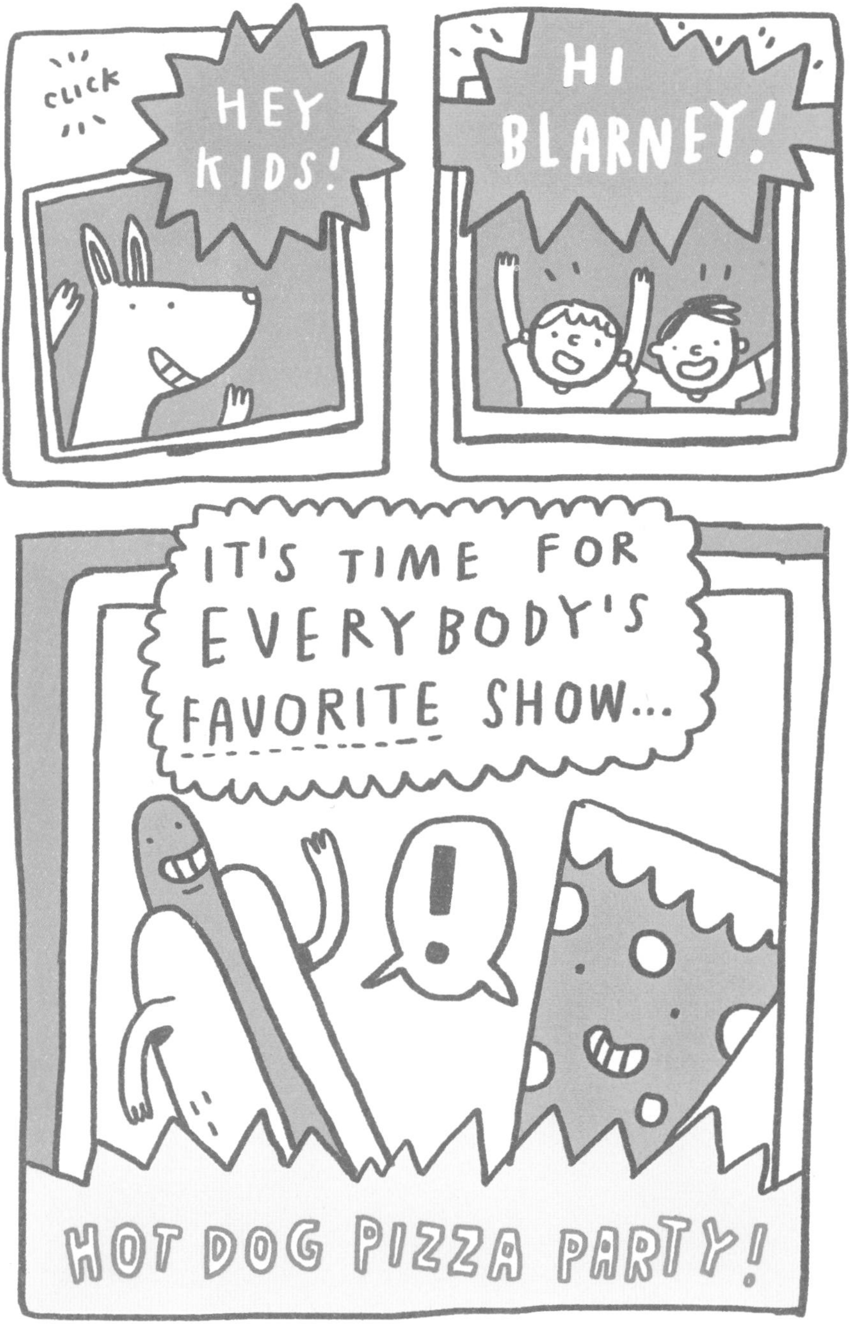
CLICK
HEY KIDS!
HI BLARNEY!
IT'S TIME FOR EVERYBODY'S FAVORITE SHOW...
!
HOT DOG PIZZA PARTY!

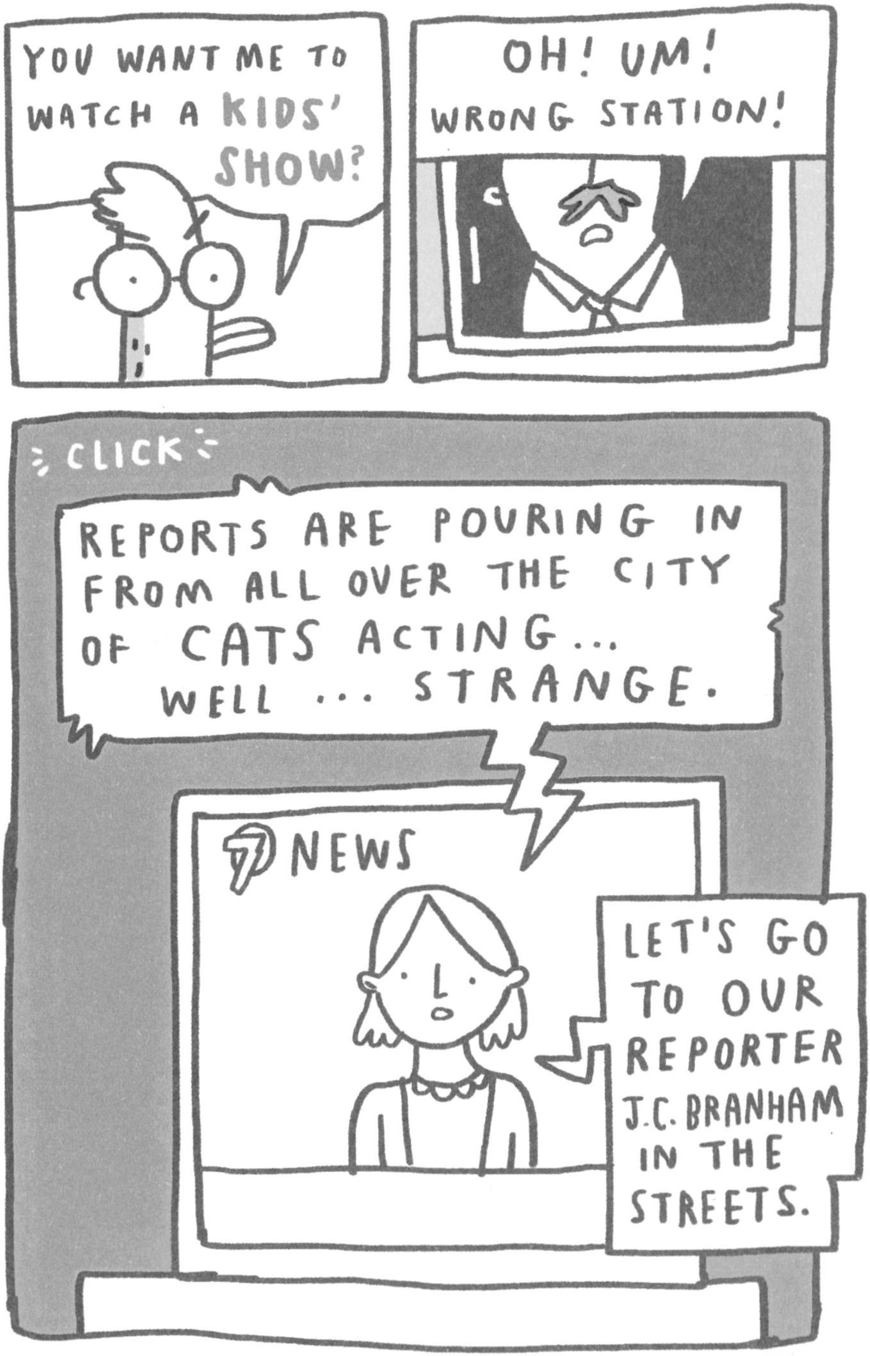
YOU WANT ME TO WATCH A KIDS' SHOW?
OH! UM! WRONG STATION!
CLICK
REPORTS ARE POURING IN FROM ALL OVER THE CITY OF CATS ACTING... WELL ... STRANGE.
NEWS
LET'S GO TO OUR REPORTER J.C. BRANHAM IN THE STREETS.

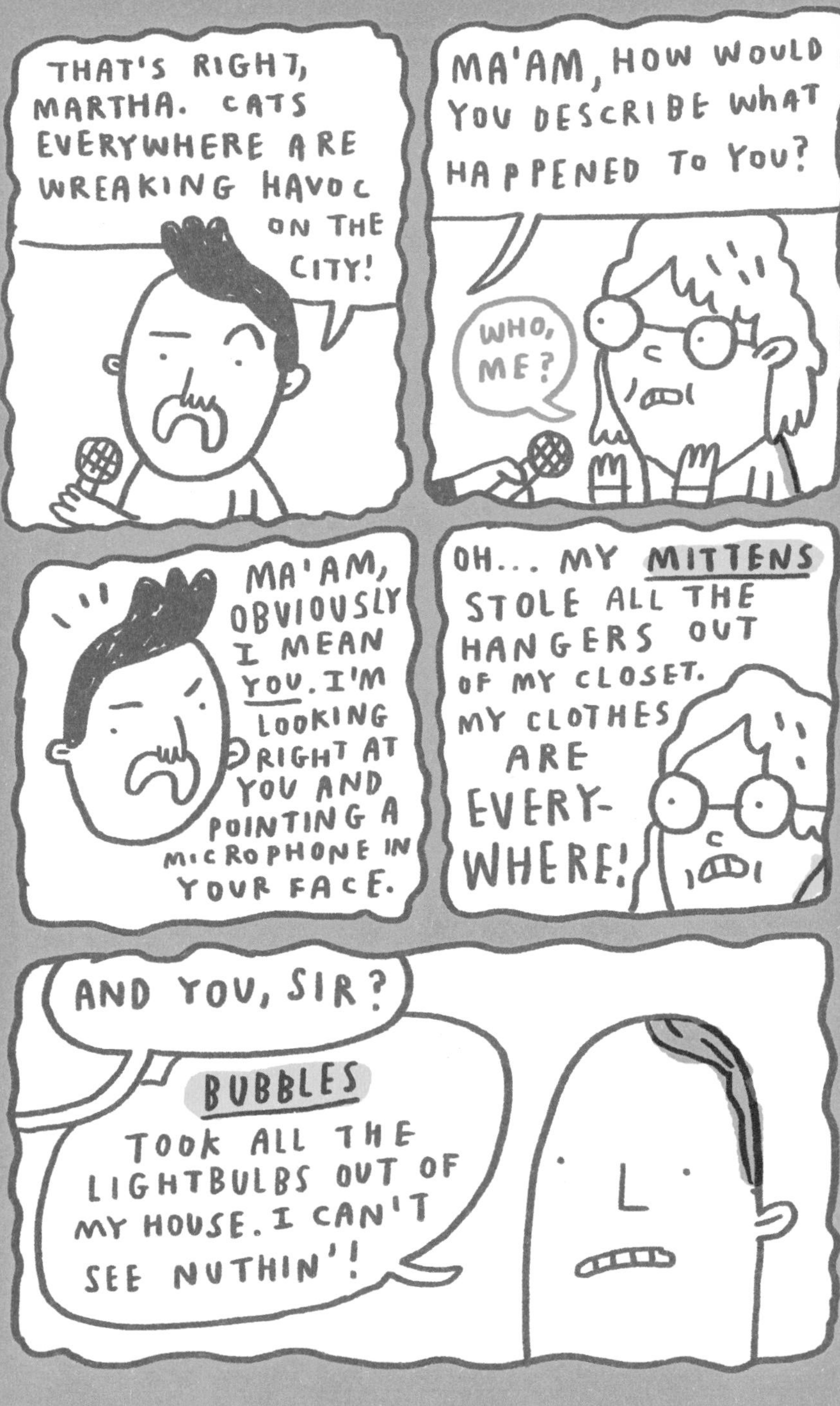
THAT'S RIGHT, MARTHA. CATS EVERYWHERE ARE WREAKING HAVOC ON THE CITY!
MA'AM, HOW WOULD YOU DESCRIBE WHAT HAPPENED TO YOU?
WHO, ME?
MA'AM, OBVIOUSLY I MEAN YOU. I'M LOOKING RIGHT AT YOU AND POINTING A MICROPHONE IN YOUR FACE.
OH... MY MITTENS STOLE ALL THE HANGERS OUT OF MY CLOSET. MY CLOTHES ARE EVERY-WHERE!
AND YOU, SIR?
BUBBLES TOOK ALL THE LIGHTBULBS OUT OF MY HOUSE. I CAN'T SEE NUTHIN'!

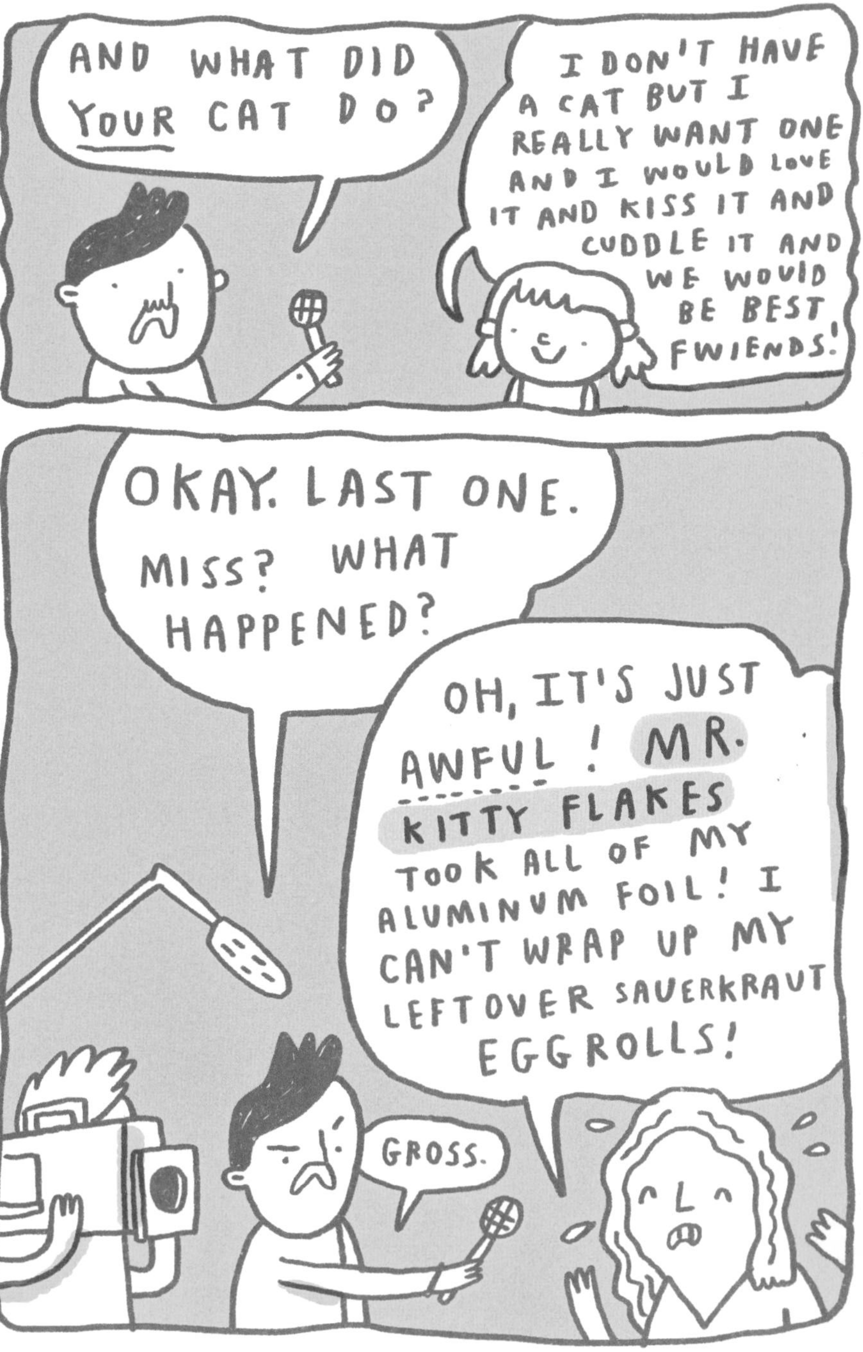
AND WHAT DID YOUR CAT DO?
I DON'T HAVE A CAT BUT I REALLY WANT ONE AND I WOULD LOVE IT AND KISS IT AND CUDDLE IT AND WE WOUID BE BEST FWIENDS!
OKAY. LAST ONE. MISS? WHAT HAPPENED?
OH, IT'S JUST AWFUL! MR. KITTY FLAKES TOOK ALL OF MY ALUMINUM FOIL! I CAN'T WRAP UP MY LEFTOVER SAUERKRAUT EGGROLLS!
GROSS.

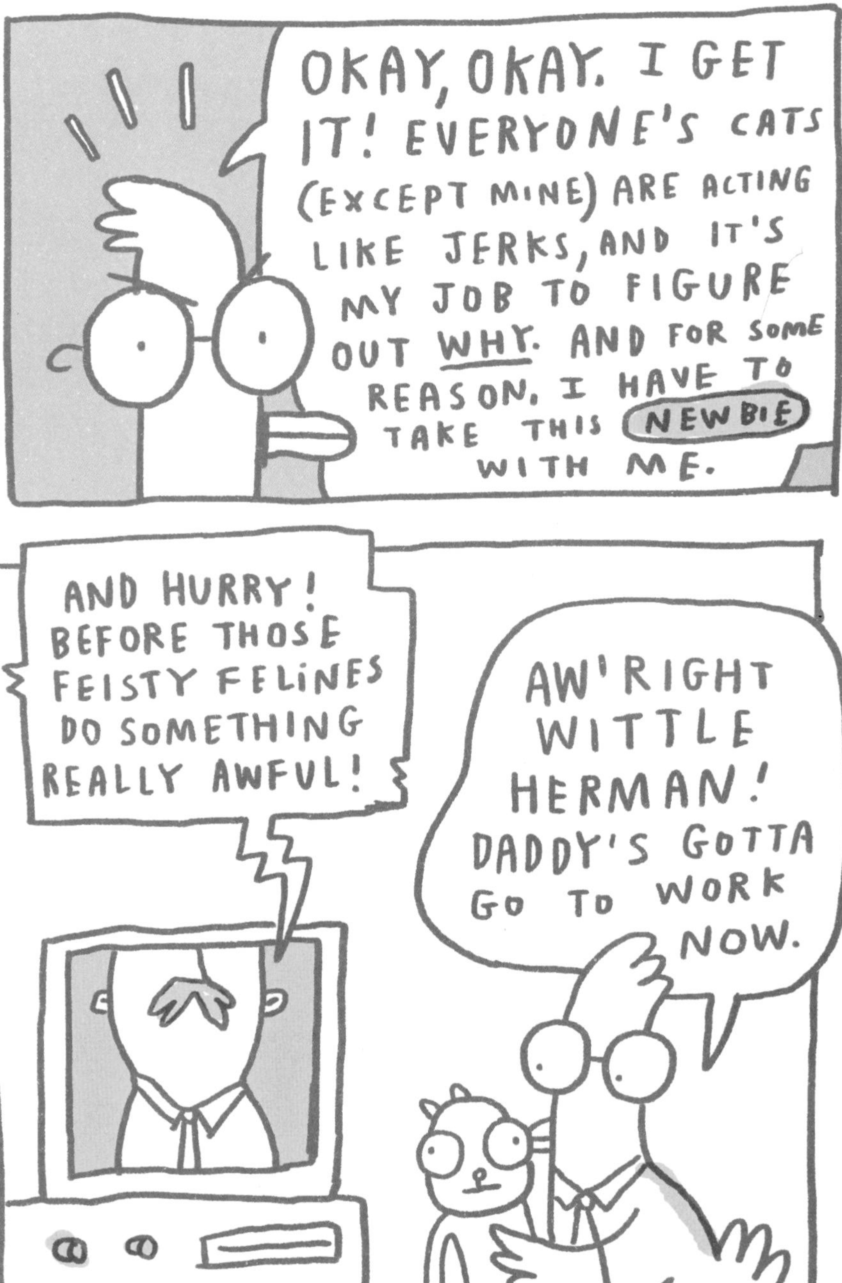
OKAY, OKAY. I GET IT! EVERYONE'S CATS (EXCEPT MINE) ARE ACTING LIKE JERKS, AND IT'S MY JOB TO FIGURE OUT WHY. AND FOR SOME REASON, I HAVE TO TAKE THIS NEWBIE WITH ME.
AND HURRY! BEFORE THOSE FEISTY FELINES DO SOMETHING REALLY AWFUL!
AW'RIGHT WITTLE HERMAN! DADDY'S GOTTA GO TO WORK NOW.

BE SURE TO GRAB SOME SUPPLIES FROM THE GEAR CLOSET!

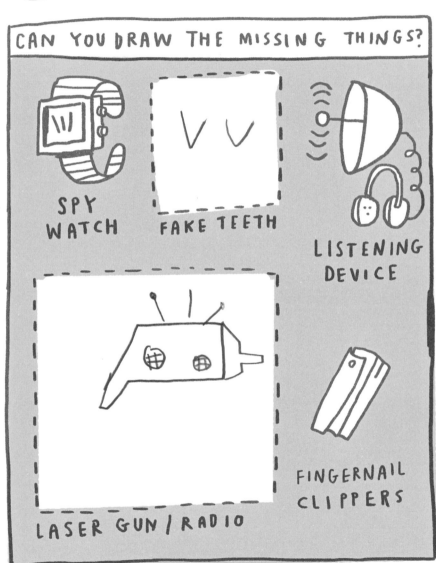

CAN YOU DRAW THE MISSING THINGS?

SPY WATCH

FAKE TEETH

LISTENING DEVICE

LASER GUN / RADIO

FINGERNAIL CLIPPERS

WHAT ELSE SHOULD WE BRING?

my brother

DON'T FORGET THE MOST IMPORTANT THING:
SUN BLOCK!
BEACH DUCK
BLOCKS UV RAYS
SPF 250
WATER PROOF

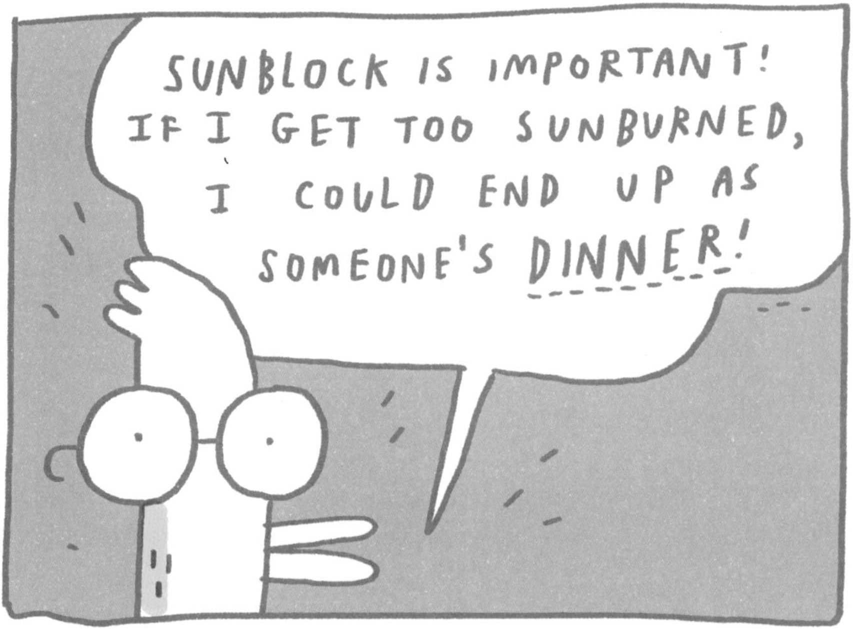
SUNBLOCK IS IMPORTANT! IF I GET TOO SUNBURNED, I COULD END UP AS SOMEONE'S DINNER!

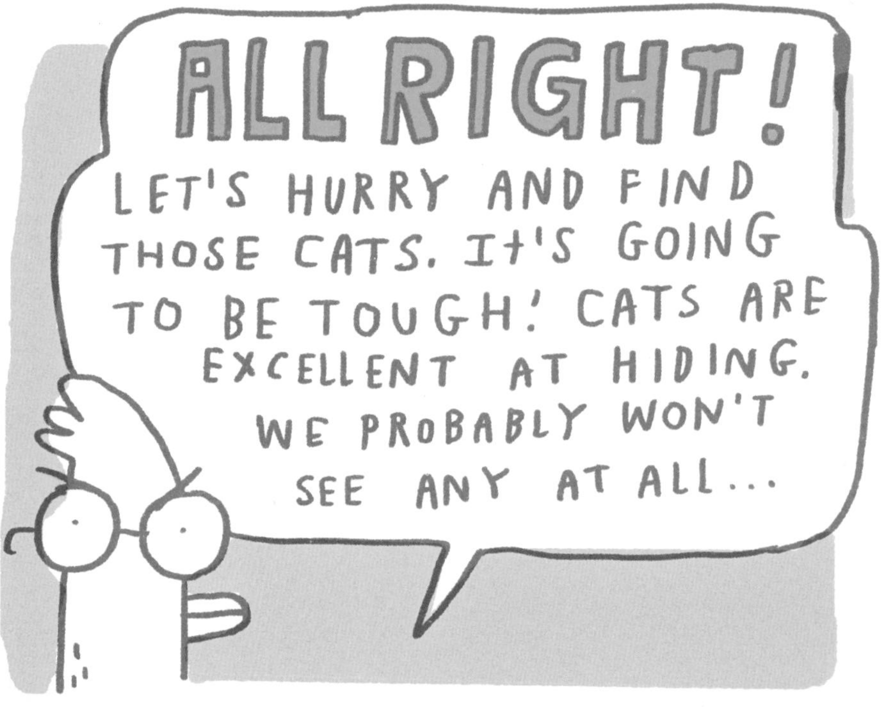
ALL RIGHT! LET'S HURRY AND FIND THOSE CATS. IT'S GOING TO BE TOUGH! CATS ARE EXCELLENT AT HIDING. WE PROBABLY WON'T SEE ANY AT ALL...

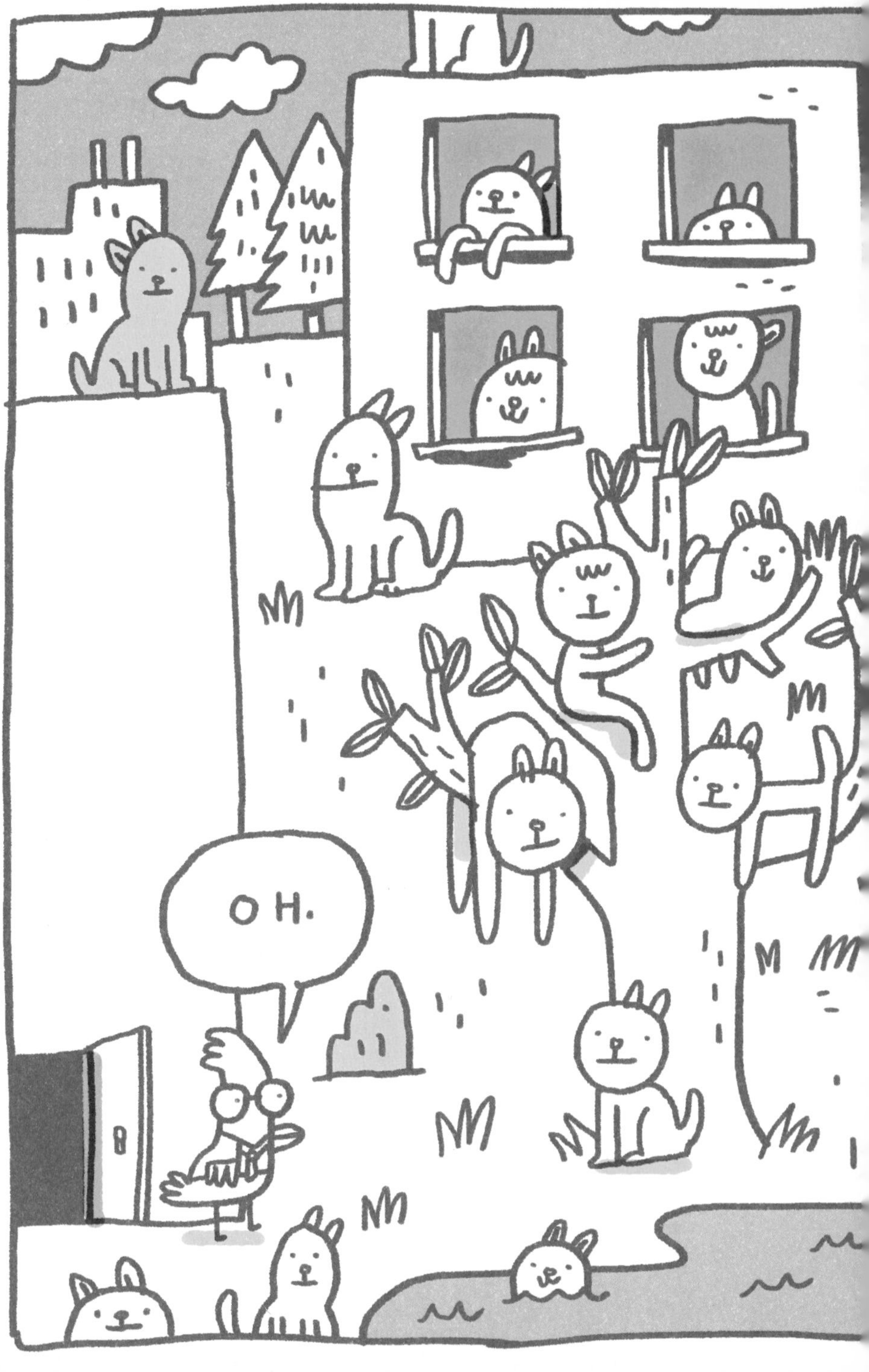
OH.

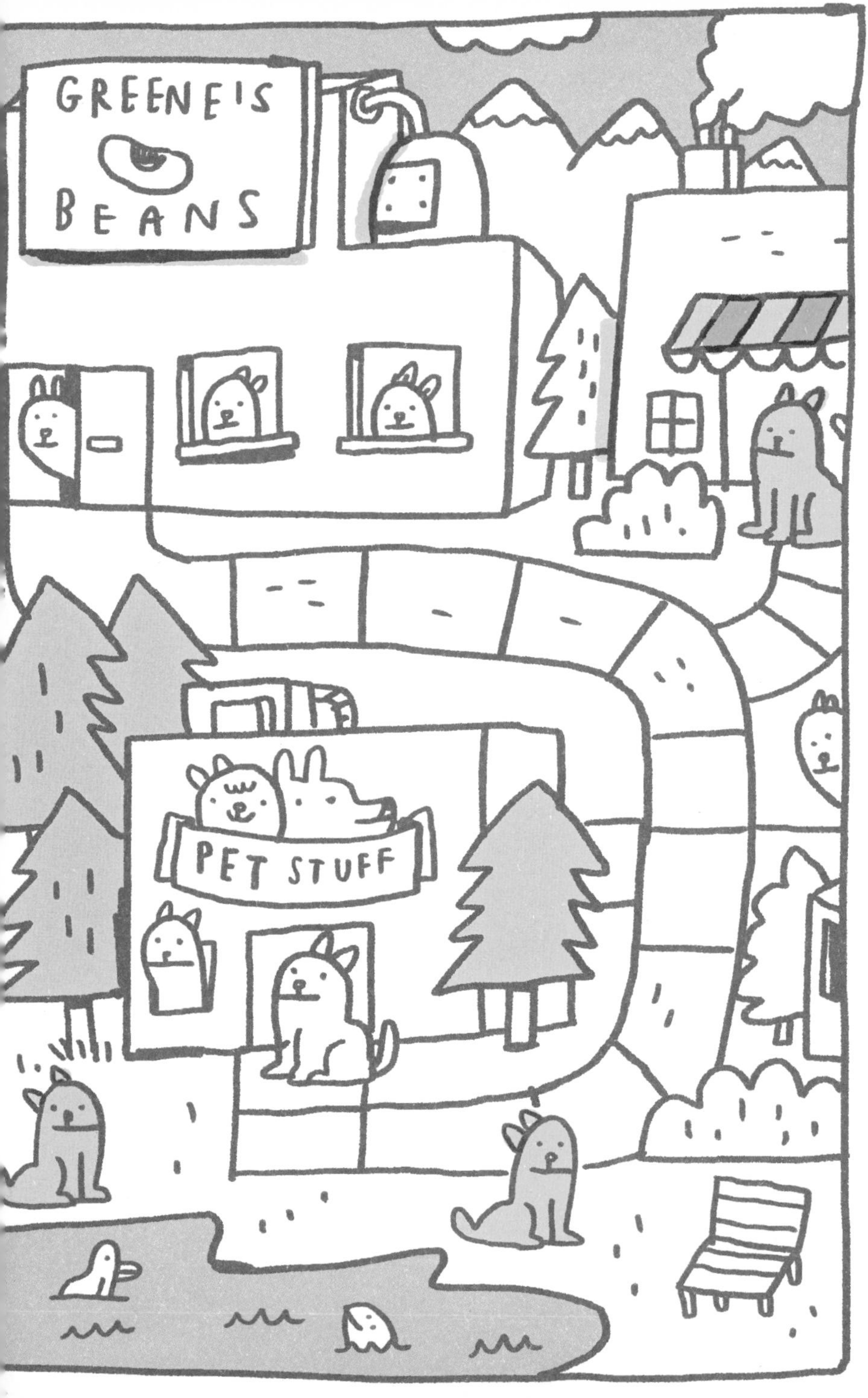
GREENE'S
BEANS
PET STUFF

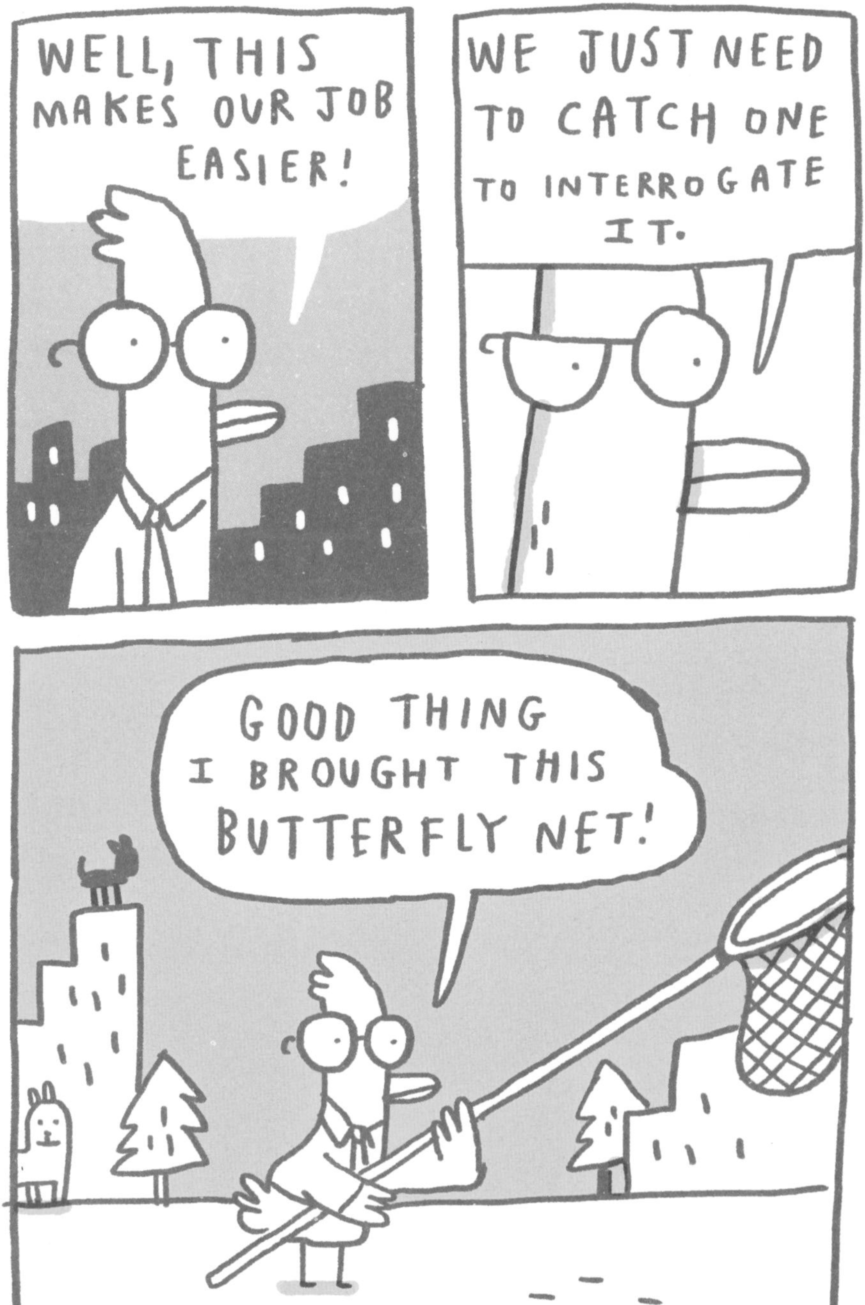
WELL, THIS MAKES OUR JOB EASIER!
WE JUST NEED TO CATCH ONE TO INTERROGATE IT.
GOOD THING I BROUGHT THIS BUTTERFLY NET!

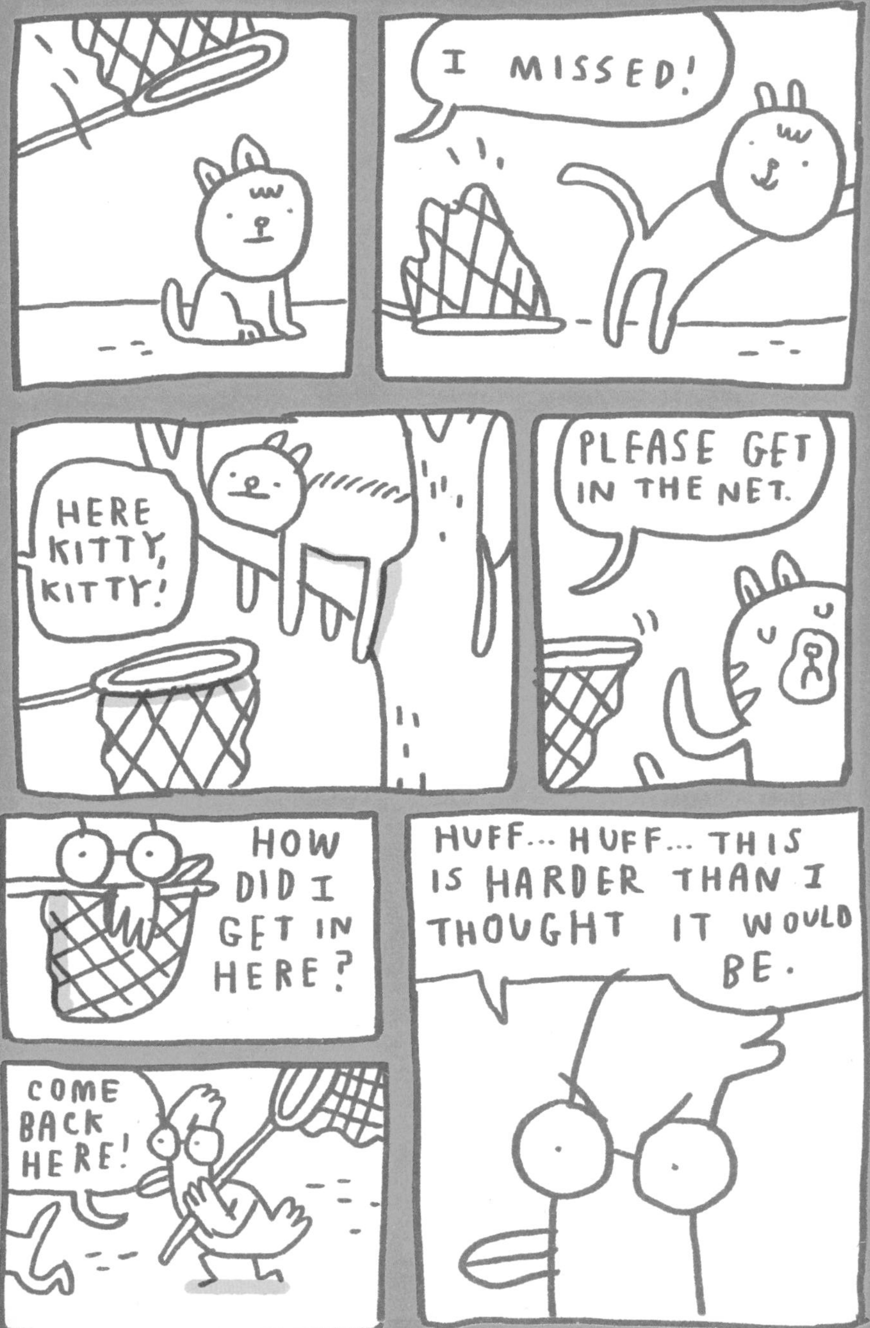
I MISSED!
HERE KITTY, KITTY!
PLEASE GET IN THE NET.
HOW DID I GET IN HERE?
COME BACK HERE!
HUFF... HUFF... THIS IS HARDER THAN I THOUGHT IT WOULD BE.

IT'S <u>YOUR TURN</u>. DRAW A
CAT TRAP! (REMEMBER: WE
DON'T WANT TO H<u>VR</u>T THEM!)

Eltro Sheild

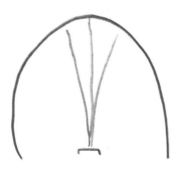

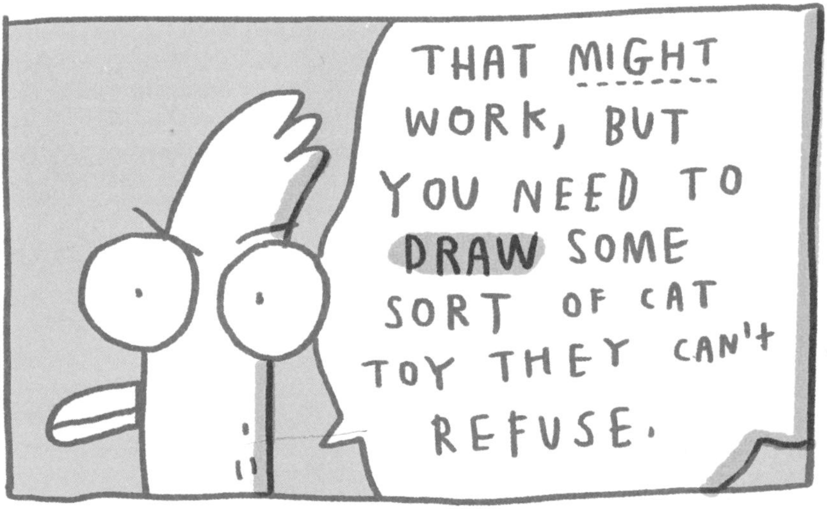
THAT MIGHT WORK, BUT YOU NEED TO DRAW SOME SORT OF CAT TOY THEY CAN'T REFUSE.

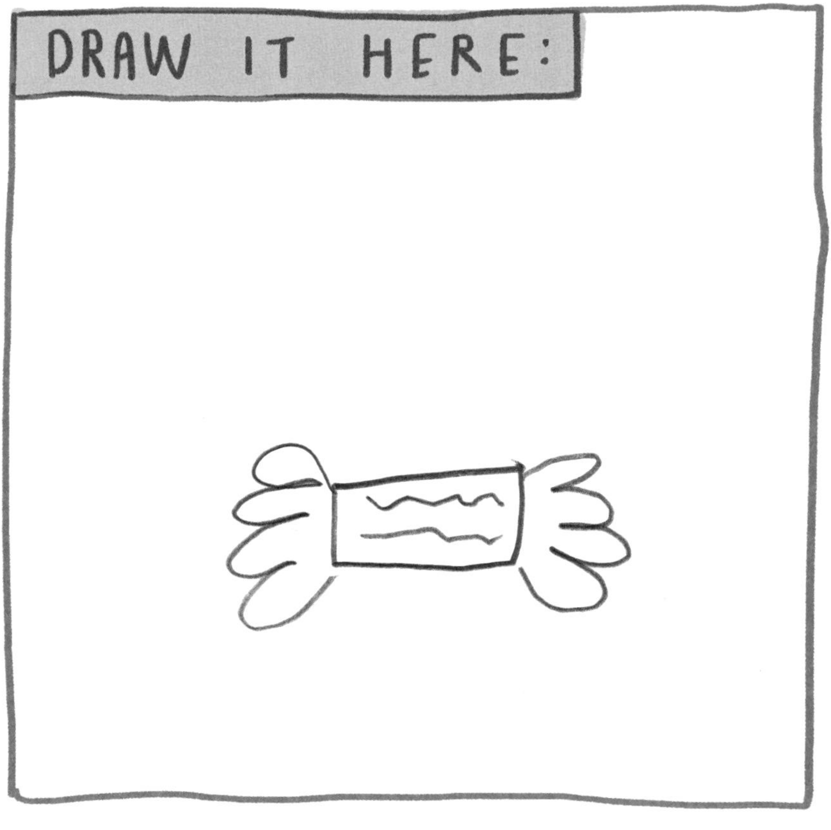
DRAW IT HERE:

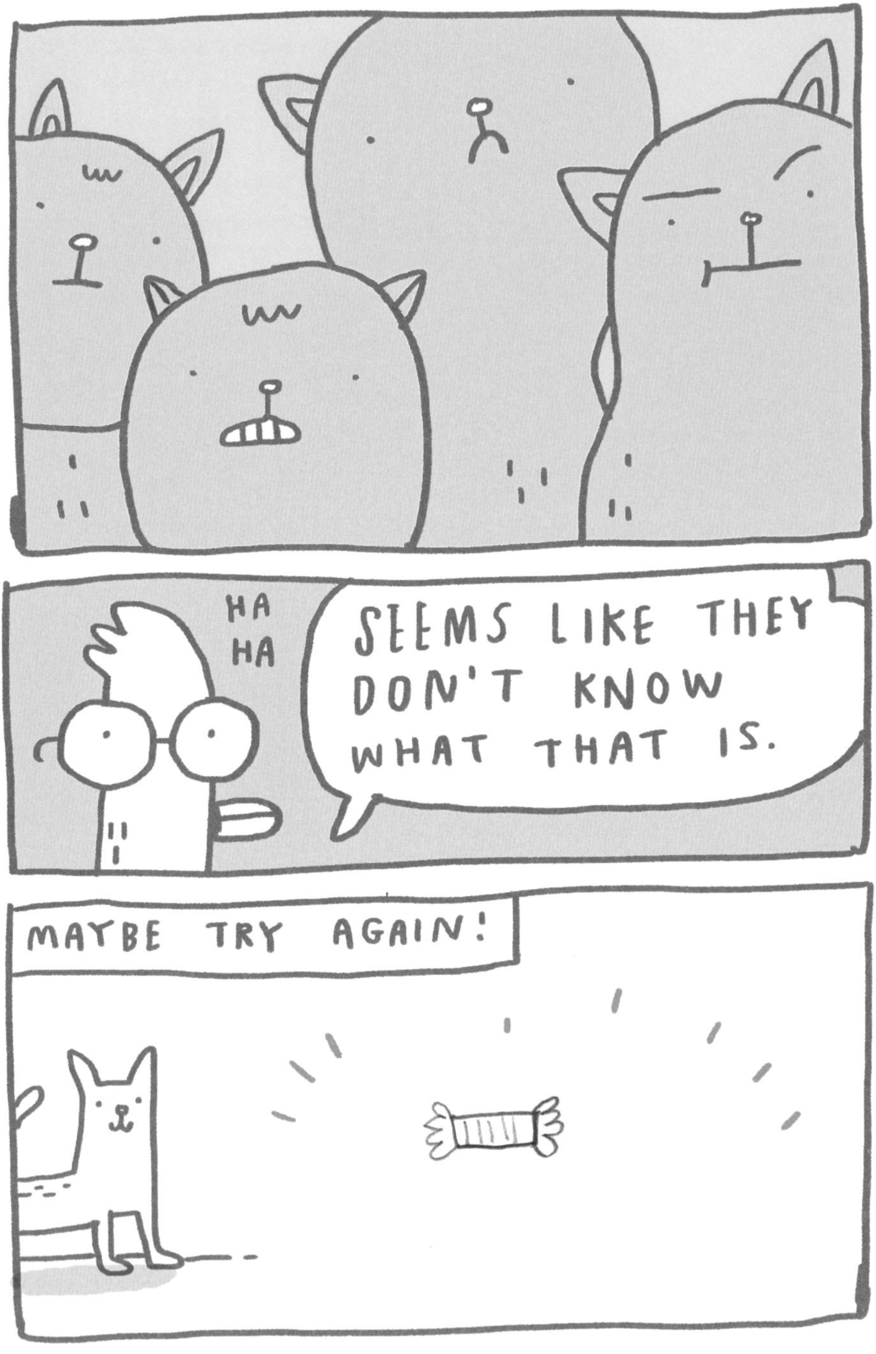
HA
HA
SEEMS LIKE THEY DON'T KNOW WHAT THAT IS.
MAYBE TRY AGAIN!

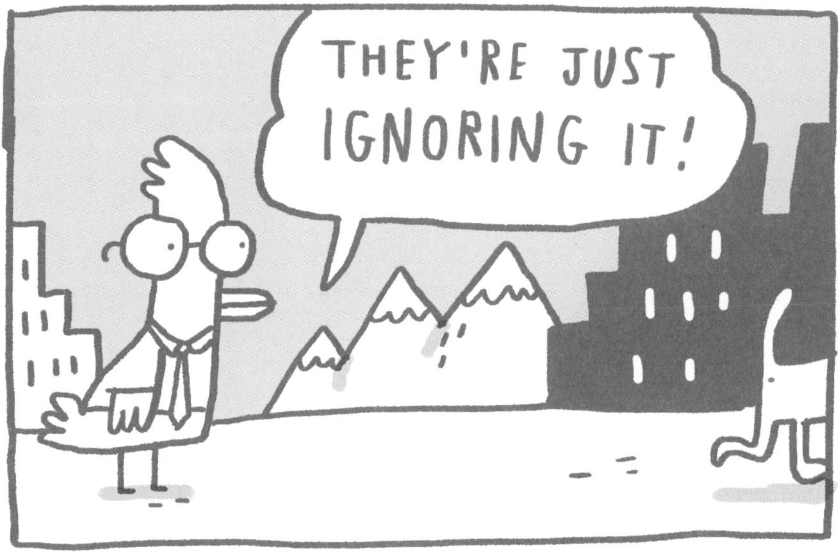
THEY'RE JUST IGNORING IT!

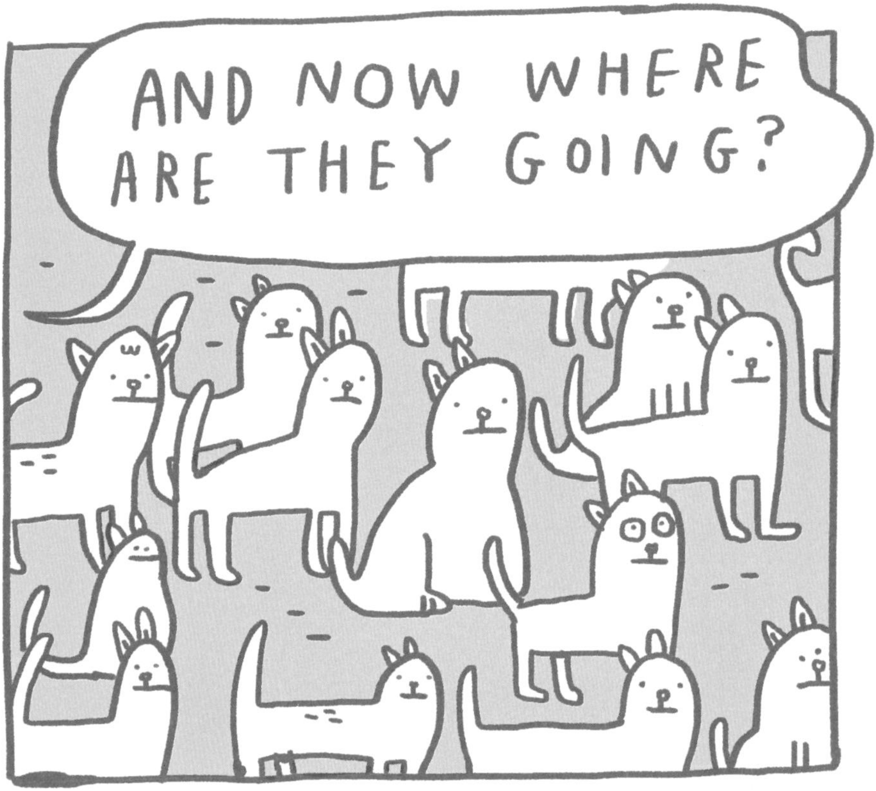
AND NOW WHERE ARE THEY GOING?

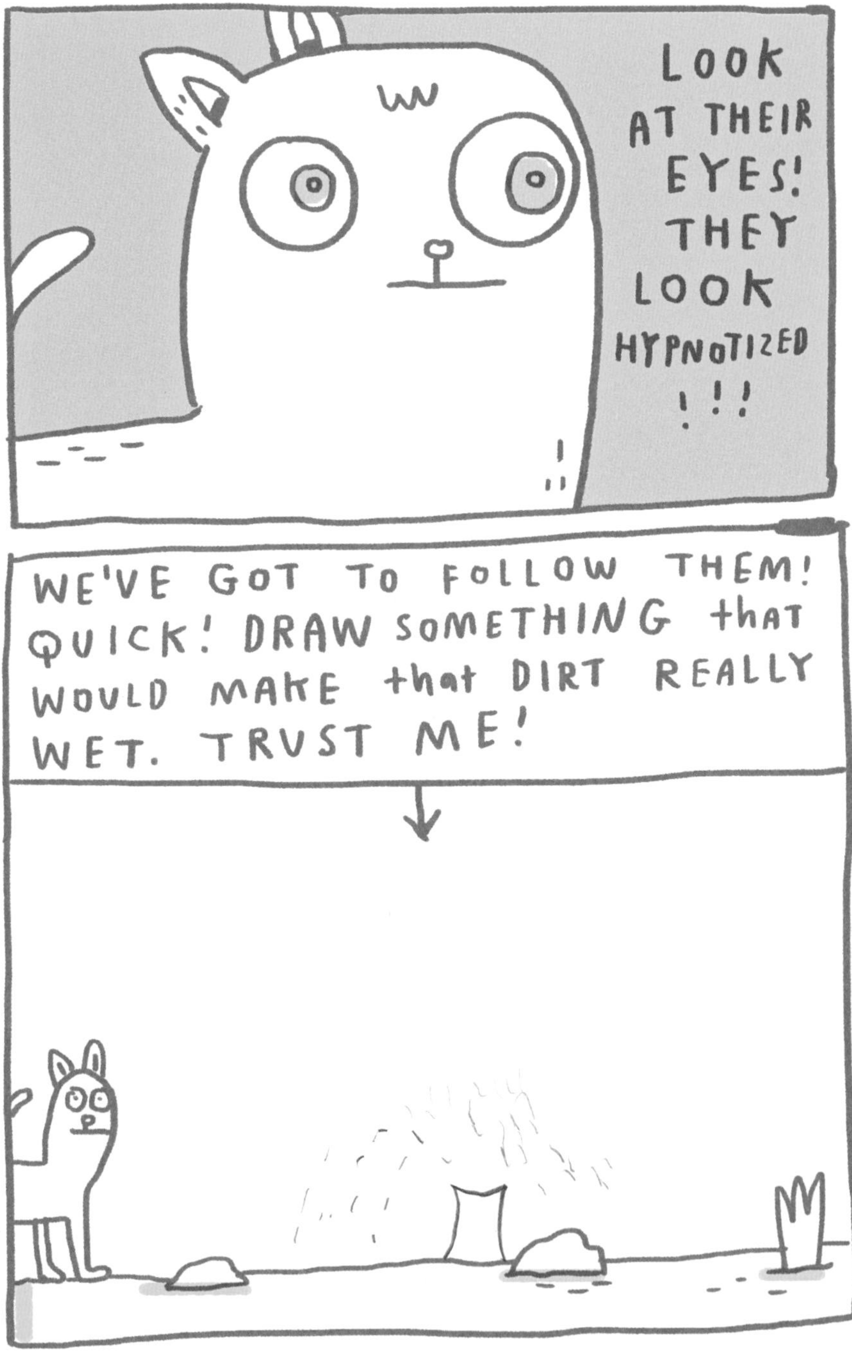
LOOK AT THEIR EYES! THEY LOOK HYPNOTIZED !!!
WE'VE GOT TO FOLLOW THEM! QUICK! DRAW SOMETHING that WOULD MAKE that DIRT REALLY WET. TRUST ME!

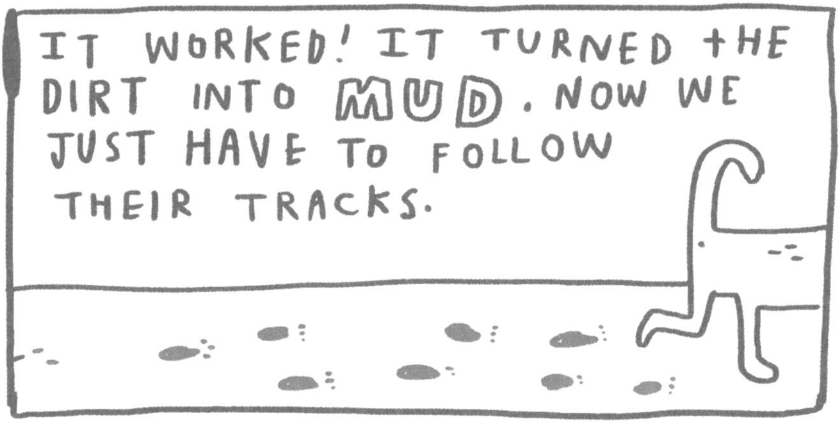
IT WORKED! IT TURNED THE DIRT INTO MUD. NOW WE JUST HAVE TO FOLLOW THEIR TRACKS.

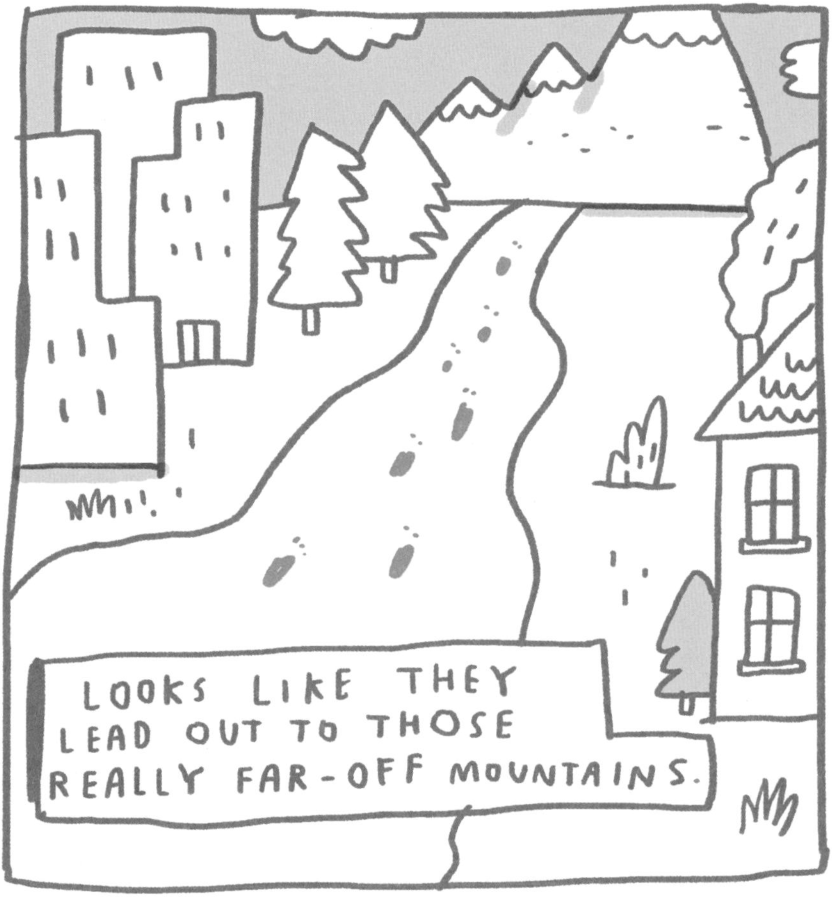
LOOKS LIKE THEY LEAD OUT TO THOSE REALLY FAR-OFF MOUNTAINS.

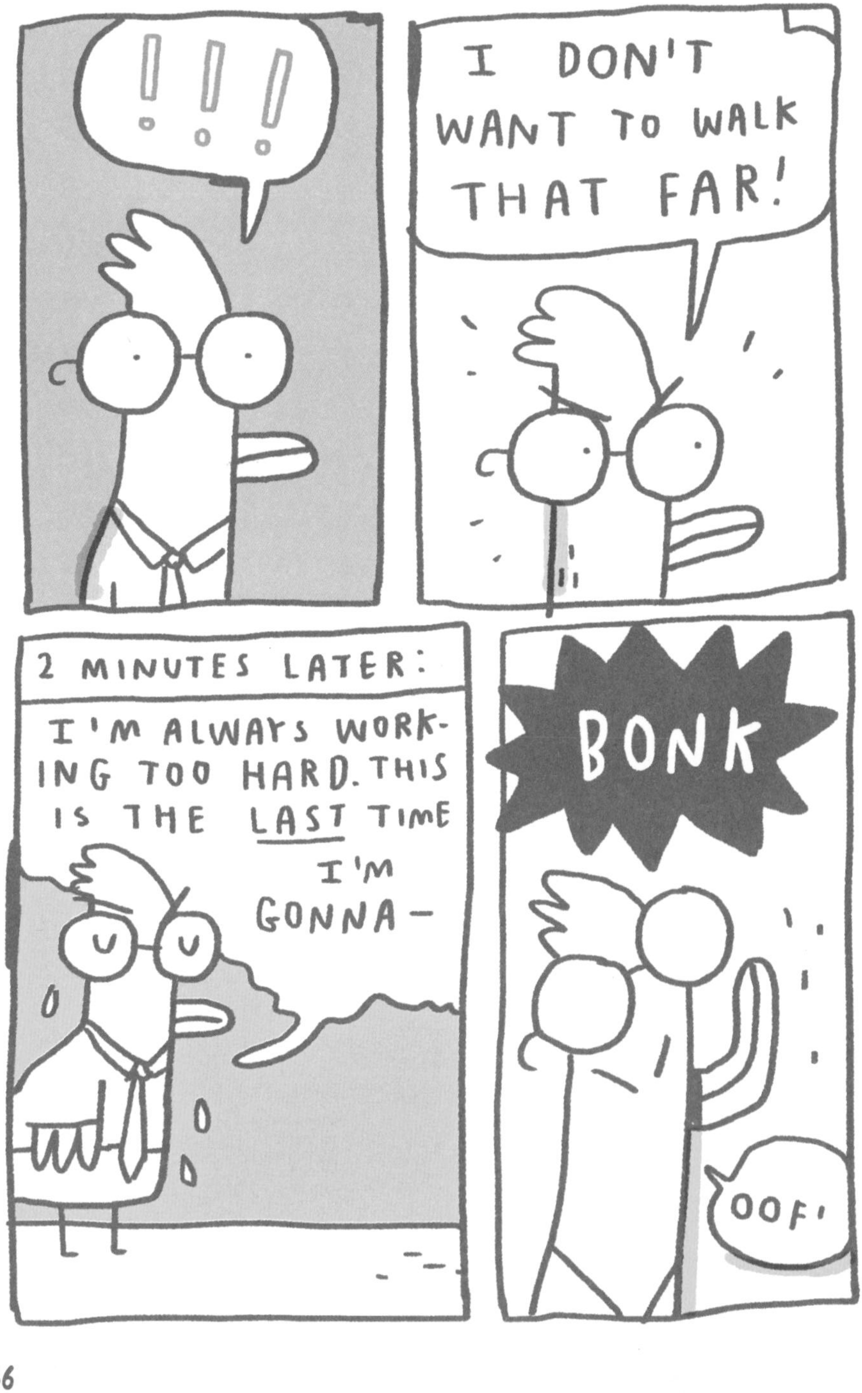
!!!
I DON'T WANT TO WALK THAT FAR!
2 MINUTES LATER:
I'M ALWAYS WORKING TOO HARD. THIS IS THE LAST TIME I'M GONNA—
BONK
OOF!

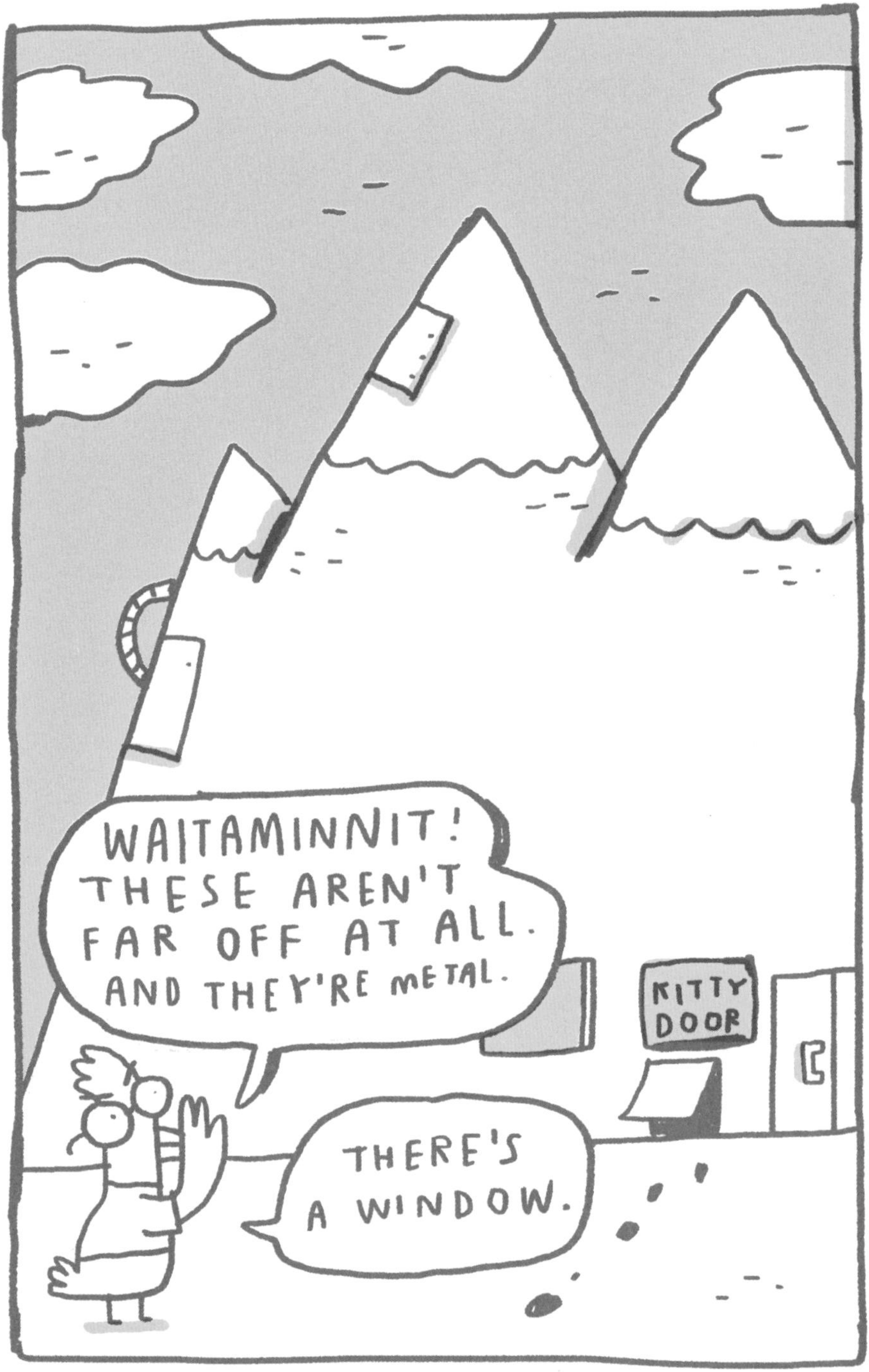
WAITAMINNIT! THESE AREN'T FAR OFF AT ALL. AND THEY'RE METAL.
KITTY DOOR
THERE'S A WINDOW.

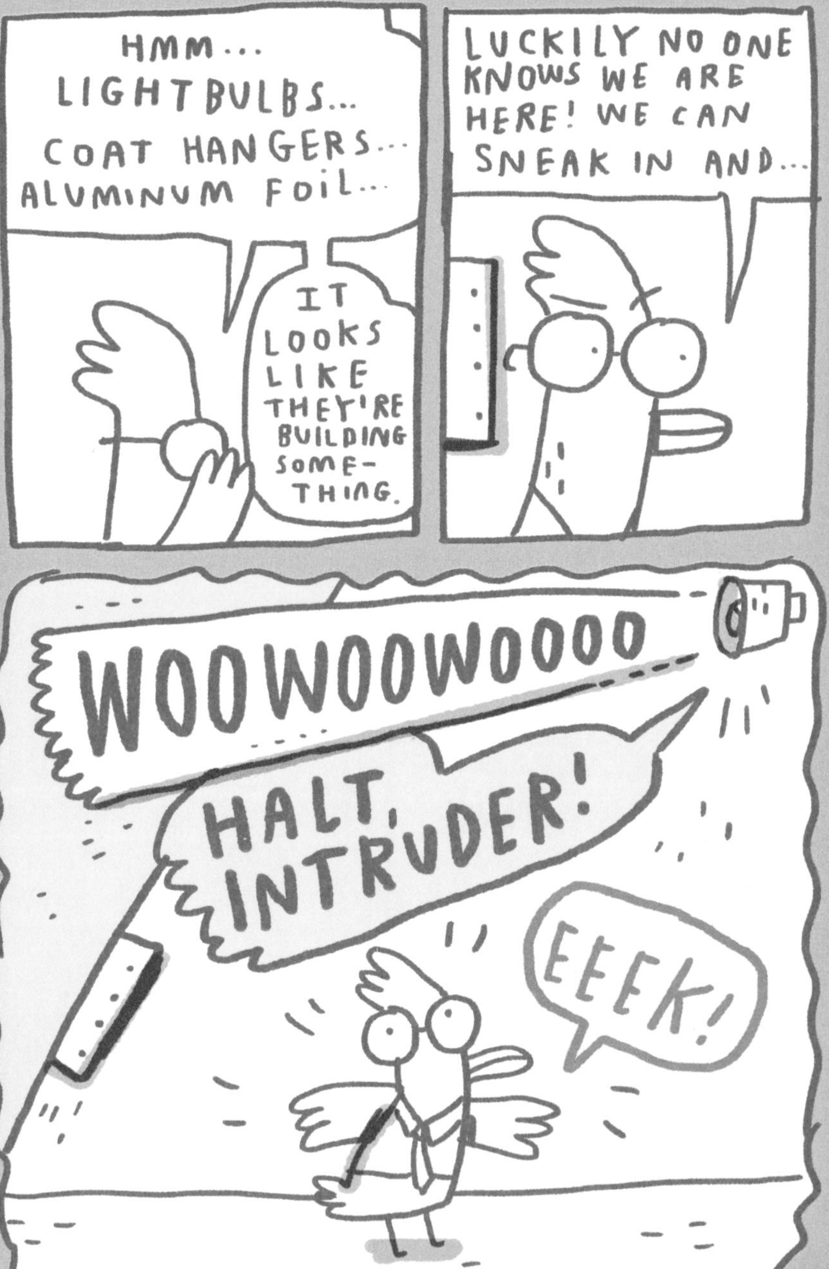
HMM...
LIGHTBULBS...
COAT HANGERS...
ALUMINUM FOIL...
IT LOOKS LIKE THEY'RE BUILDING SOME-THING.
LUCKILY NO ONE KNOWS WE ARE HERE! WE CAN SNEAK IN AND...
WOOWOOWOOOO
HALT, INTRUDER!
EEEK!

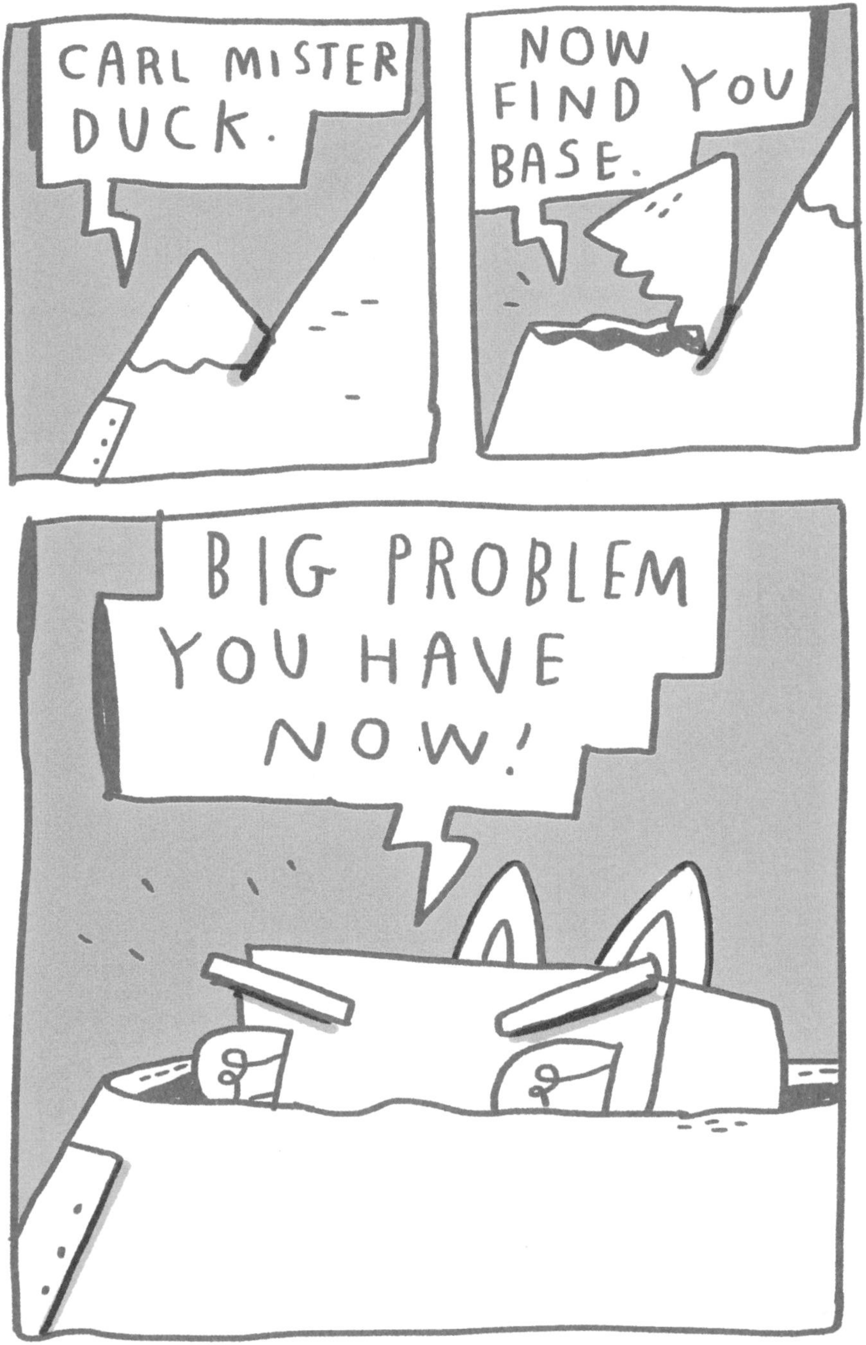
CARL MISTER DUCK.
NOW FIND YOU BASE.
BIG PROBLEM YOU HAVE NOW!

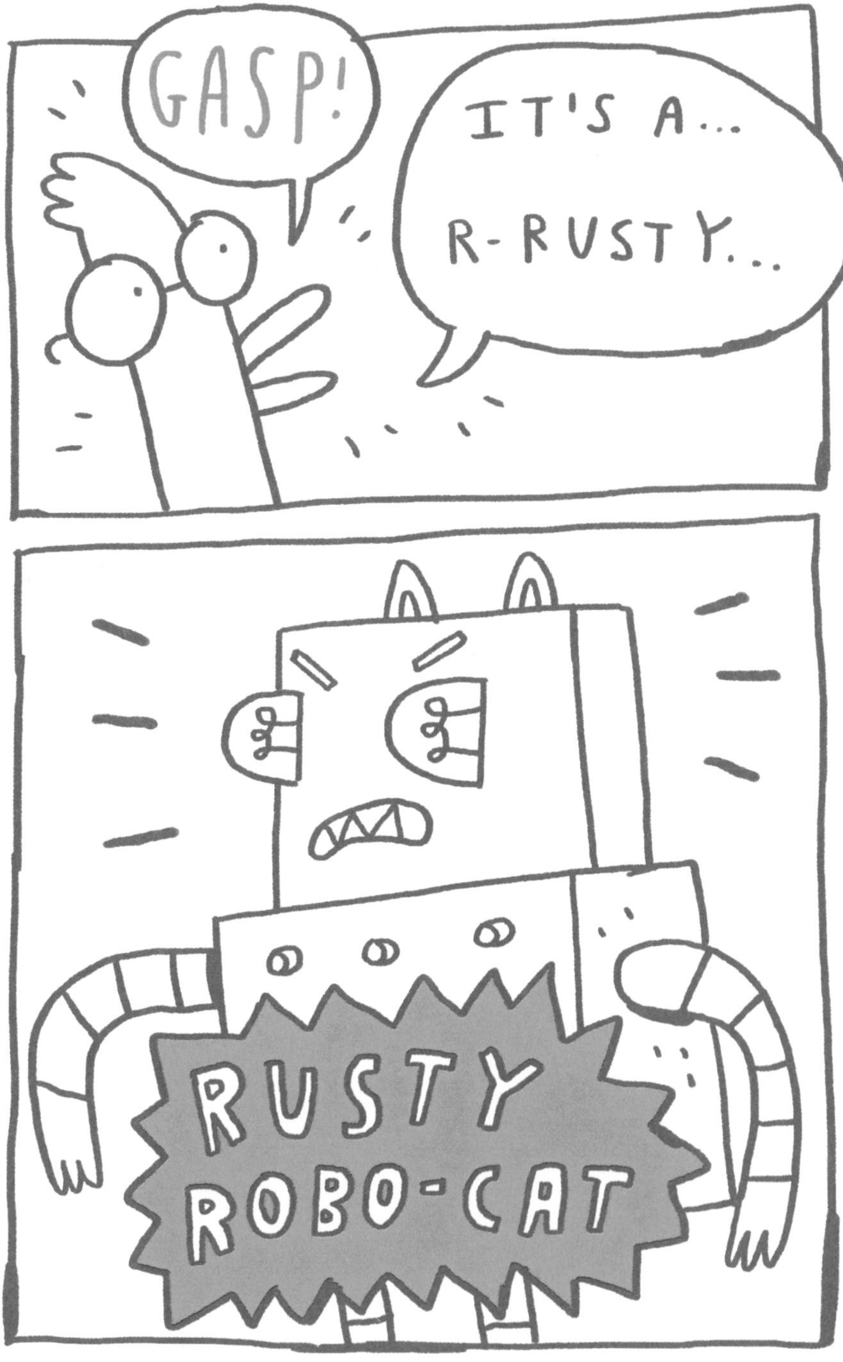
GASP!
IT'S A...
R-RUSTY...
RUSTY ROBO-CAT

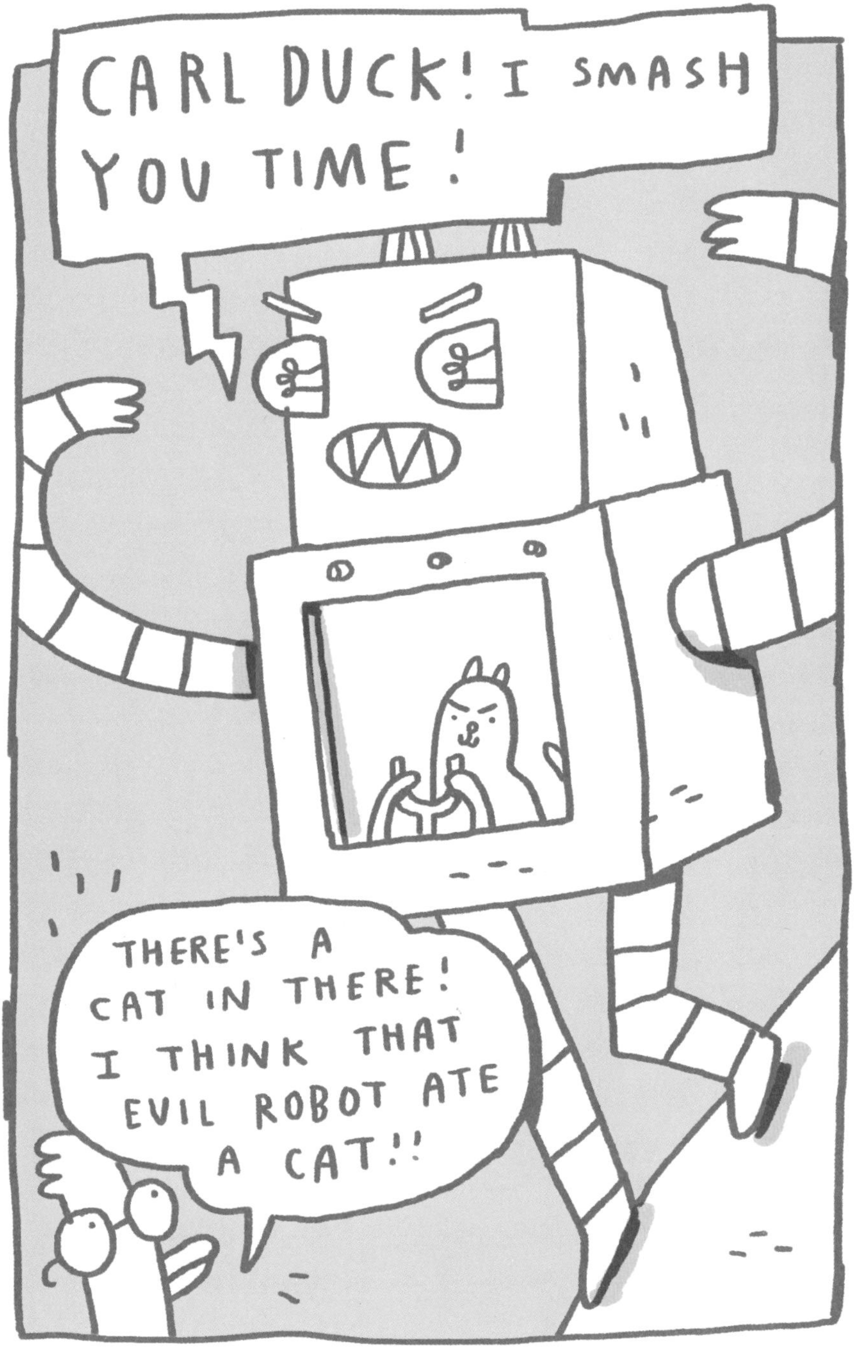
CARL DUCK! I SMASH YOU TIME!
THERE'S A CAT IN THERE! I THINK THAT EVIL ROBOT ATE A CAT!!

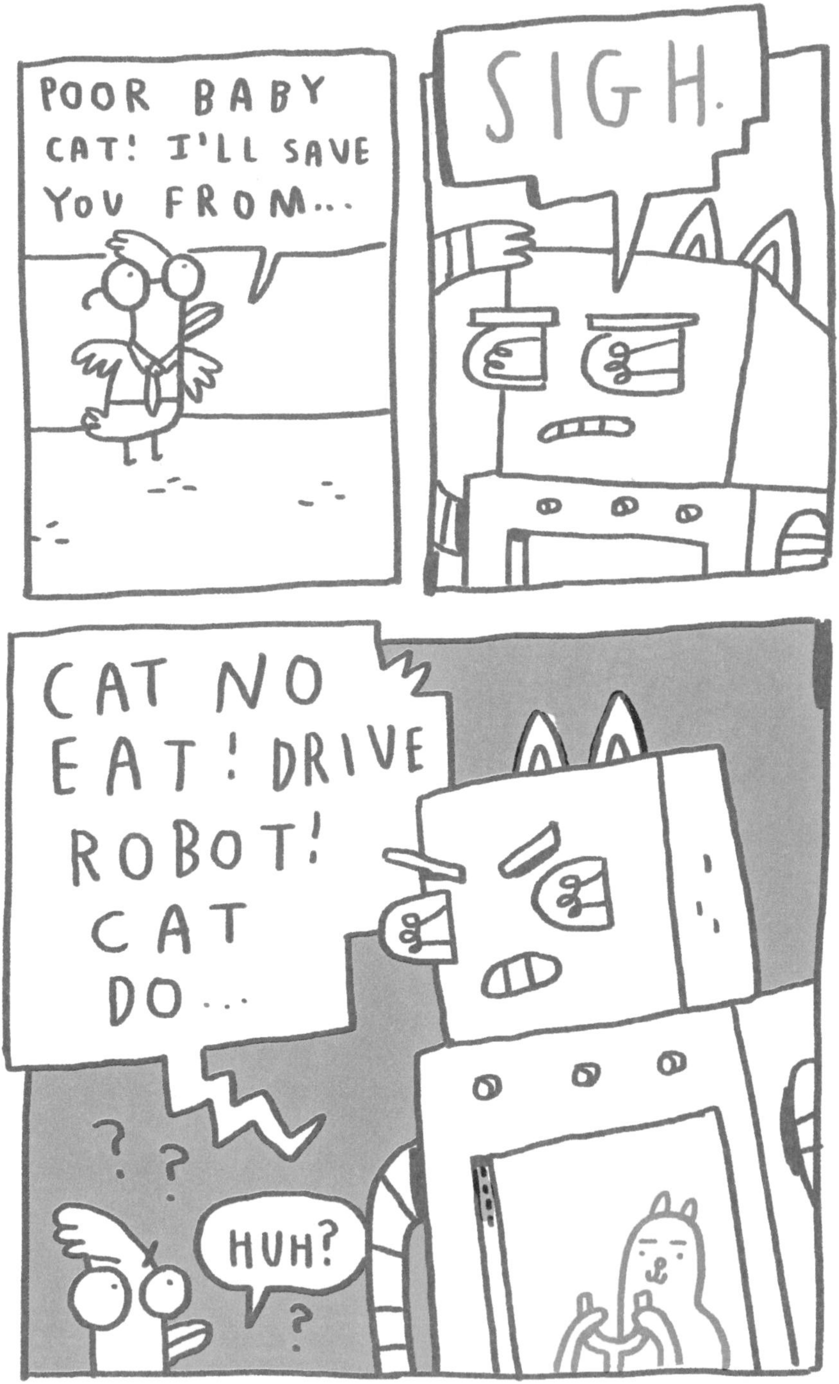
POOR BABY CAT! I'LL SAVE YOU FROM...
SIGH.
CAT NO EAT! DRIVE ROBOT! CAT DO...
HUH?

THE CAT-TO-HUMAN TRANSLATOR IS MISSING ONE CRITICAL PART. CAN YOU DRAW IT SO WE CAN UNDERSTAND WHAT IT'S SAYING?

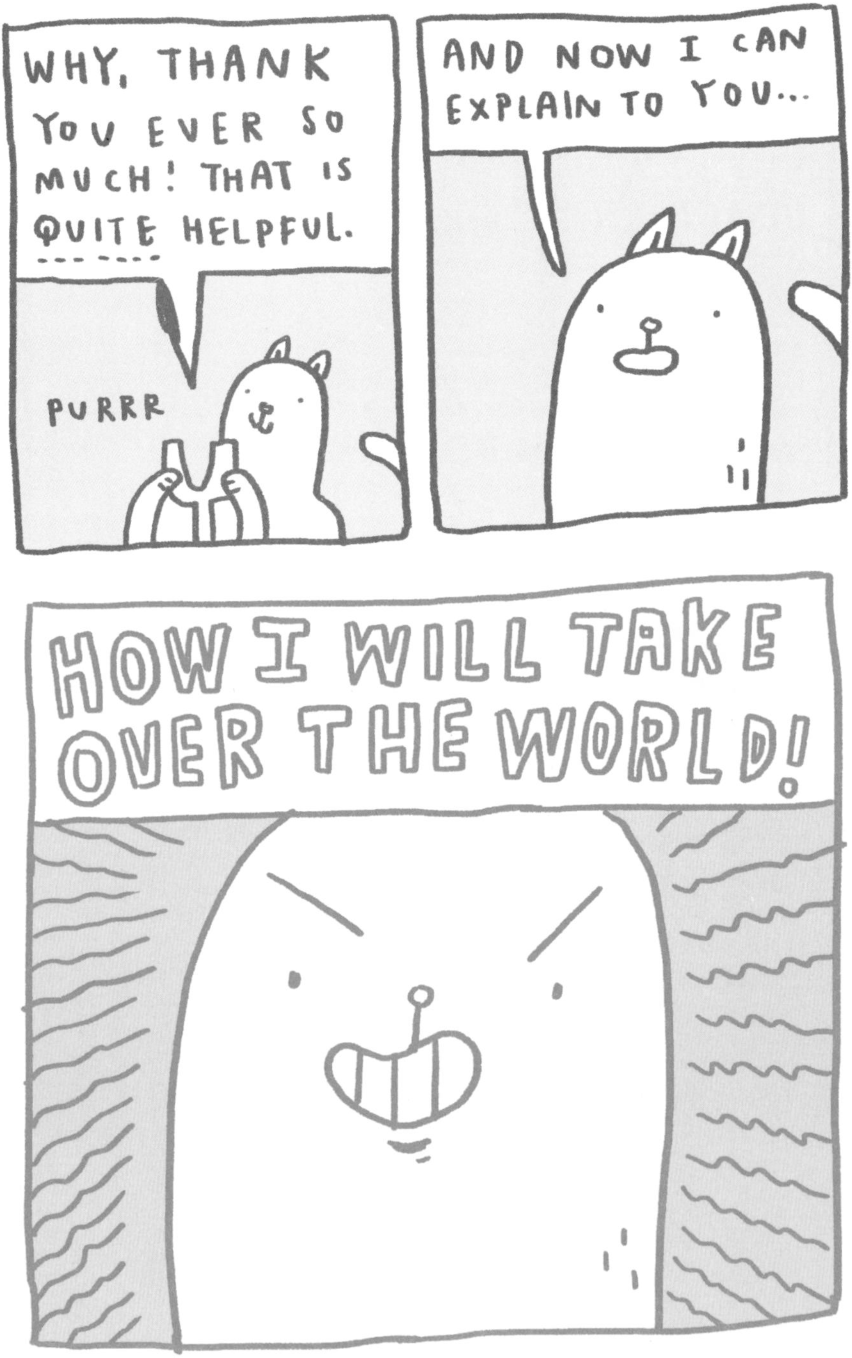
WHY, THANK YOU EVER SO MUCH! THAT IS QUITE HELPFUL.
PURRR
AND NOW I CAN EXPLAIN TO YOU...
HOW I WILL TAKE OVER THE WORLD!

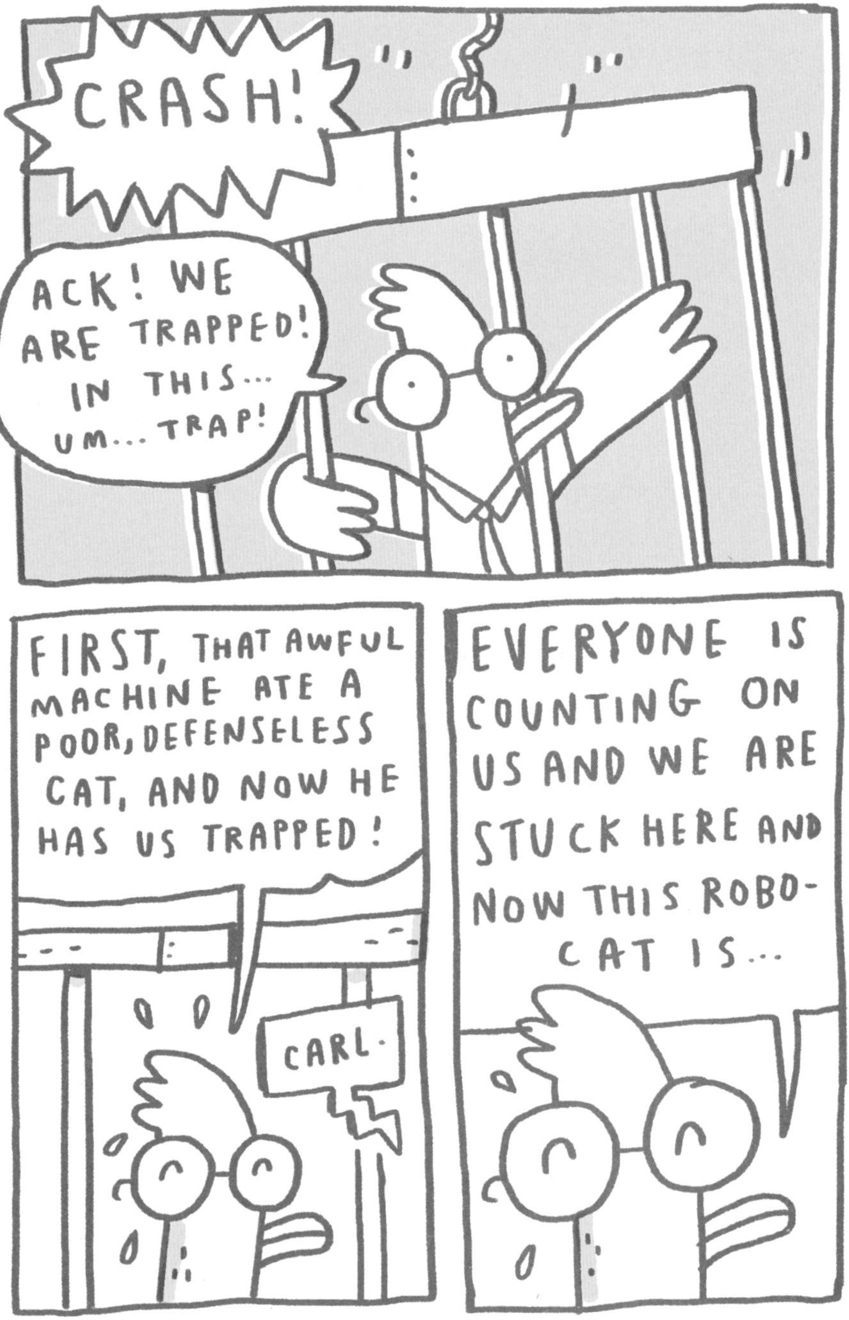
CRASH!
ACK! WE ARE TRAPPED! IN THIS... UM... TRAP!
FIRST, THAT AWFUL MACHINE ATE A POOR, DEFENSELESS CAT, AND NOW HE HAS US TRAPPED!
CARL.
EVERYONE IS COUNTING ON US AND WE ARE STUCK HERE AND NOW THIS ROBO-CAT IS...

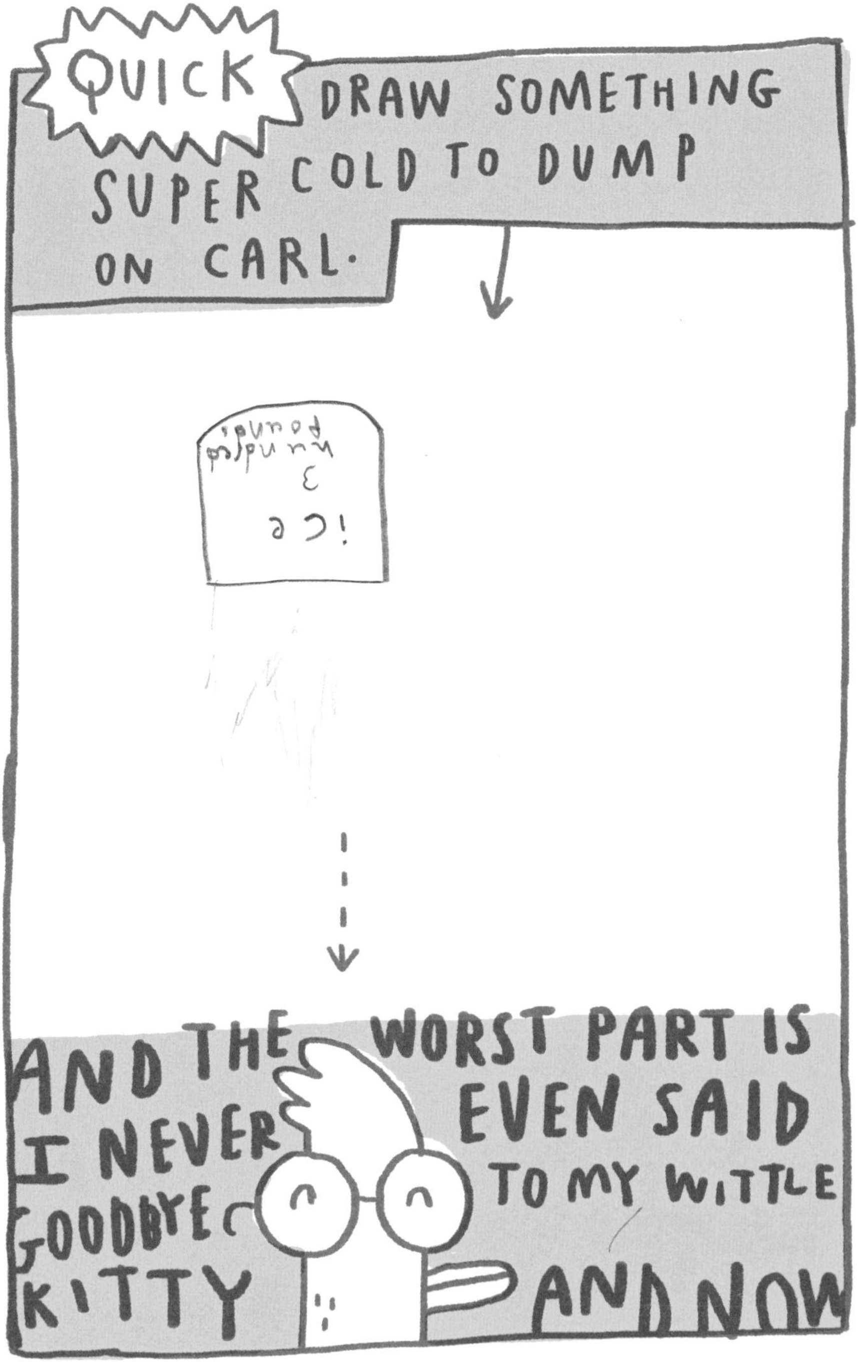
QUICK
DRAW SOMETHING SUPER COLD TO DUMP ON CARL.
AND THE WORST PART IS I NEVER EVEN SAID GOODBYE TO MY WITTLE KITTY
AND NOW

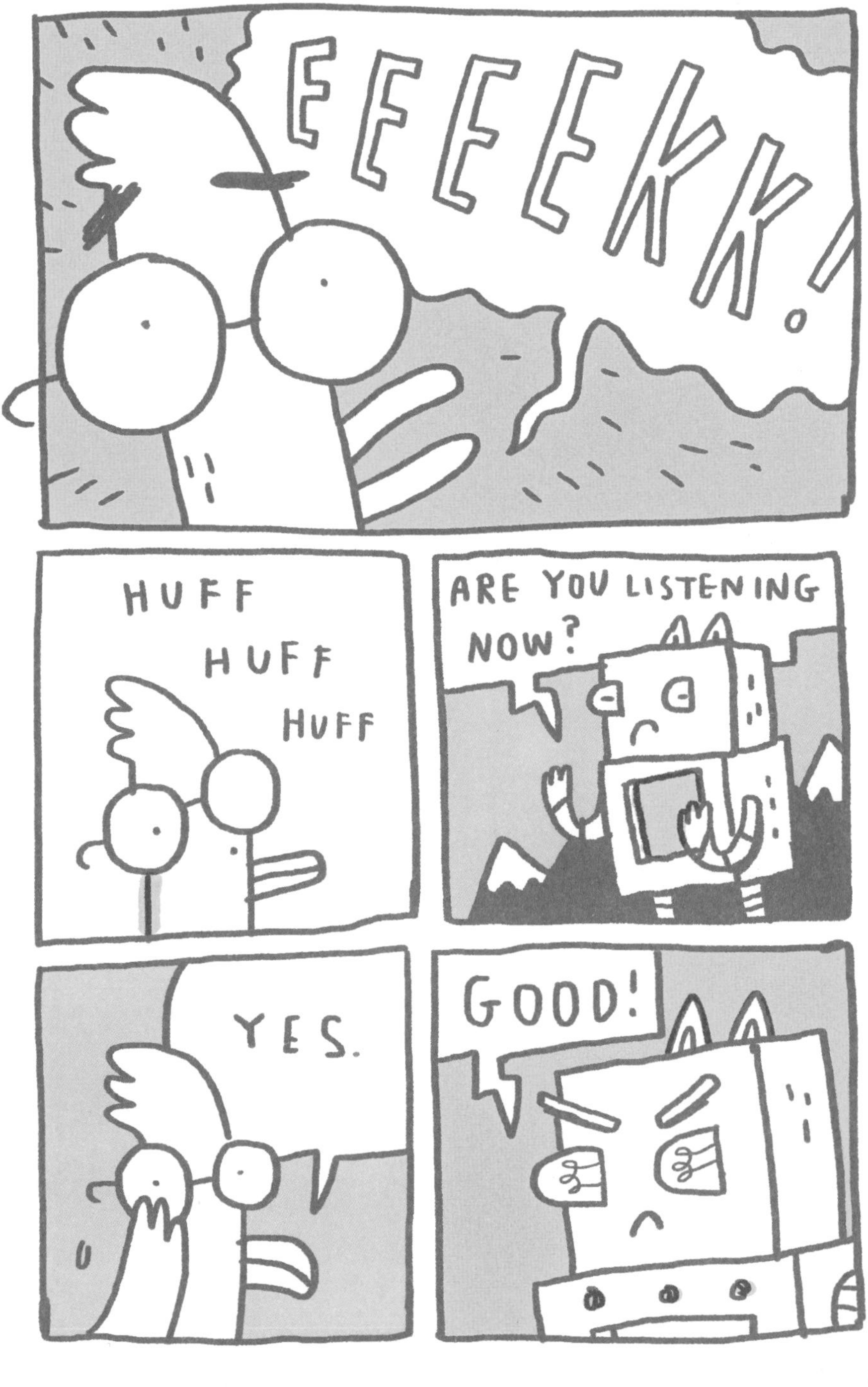
EEEEKK!
HUFF
HUFF
HUFF
ARE YOU LISTENING NOW?
YES.
GOOD!

FOR MONTHS, I HAVE LIVED HERE IN THIS FAKE MOUNTAIN HIDEOUT WHERE I HAVE SECRETLY BEEN BUILDING THIS ROBO-CAT OUT OF FOUND ODDS AND ENDS. I NEEDED MORE STUFF SO I BUILT A HYPNO-MACHINE AND TOOK CONTROL OF ALL THE CATS IN THE CITY!

THEY HAVE BEEN BRINGING ME ALL SORTS OF GREAT ROBOT-BUILDING SUPPLIES, LIKE:

COAT
HANGERS

LIGHT-
BULBS

BOLTS
AND SCREWS

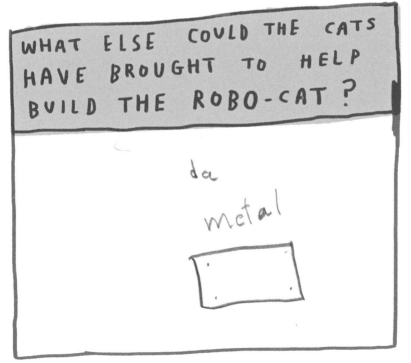

WHAT ELSE COULD THE CATS HAVE BROUGHT TO HELP BUILD THE ROBO-CAT ?

da

metal

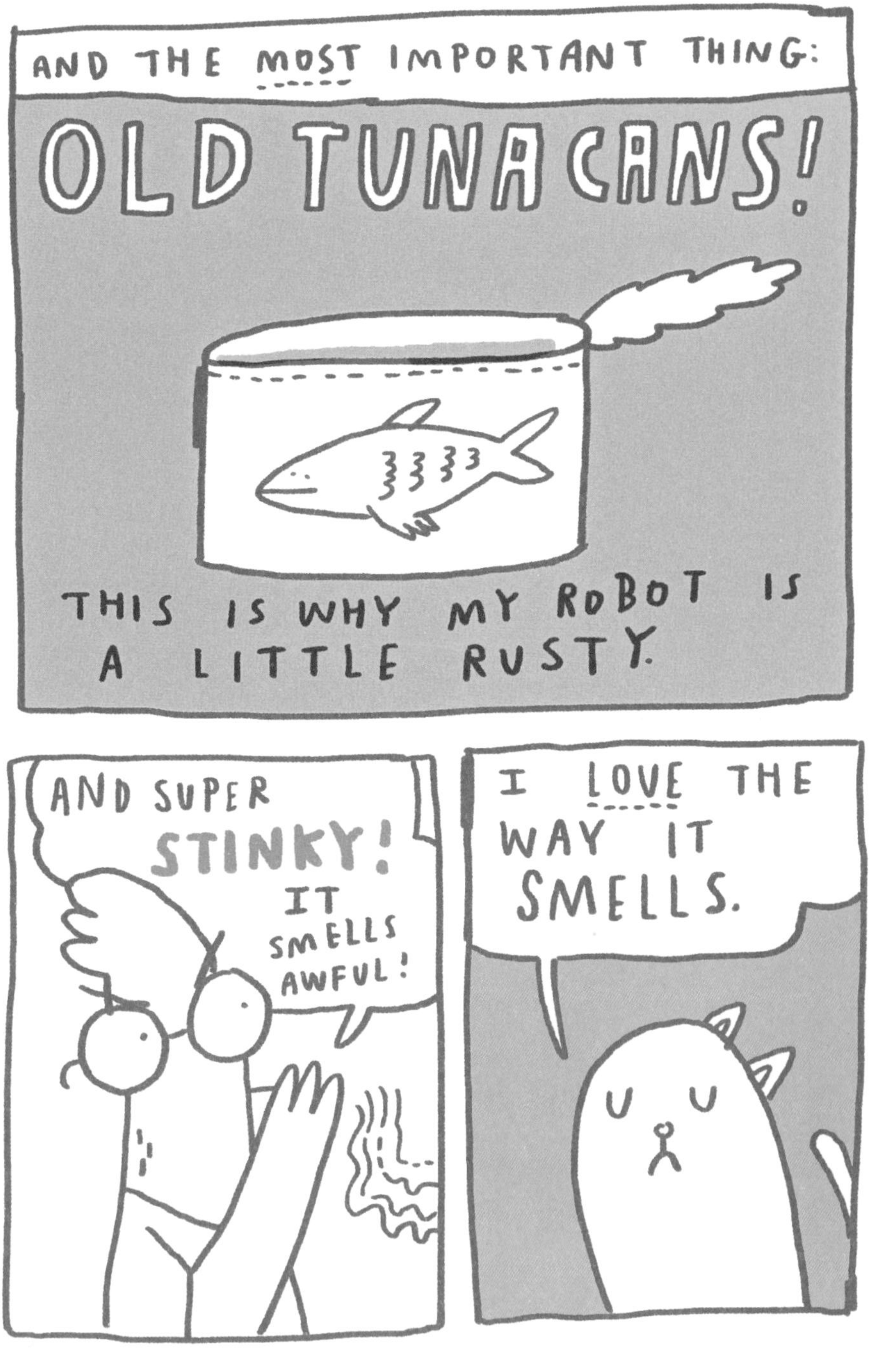
AND THE MOST IMPORTANT THING:
OLD TUNA CANS!
THIS IS WHY MY ROBOT IS A LITTLE RUSTY.
AND SUPER STINKY!
IT SMELLS AWFUL!
I LOVE THE WAY IT SMELLS.

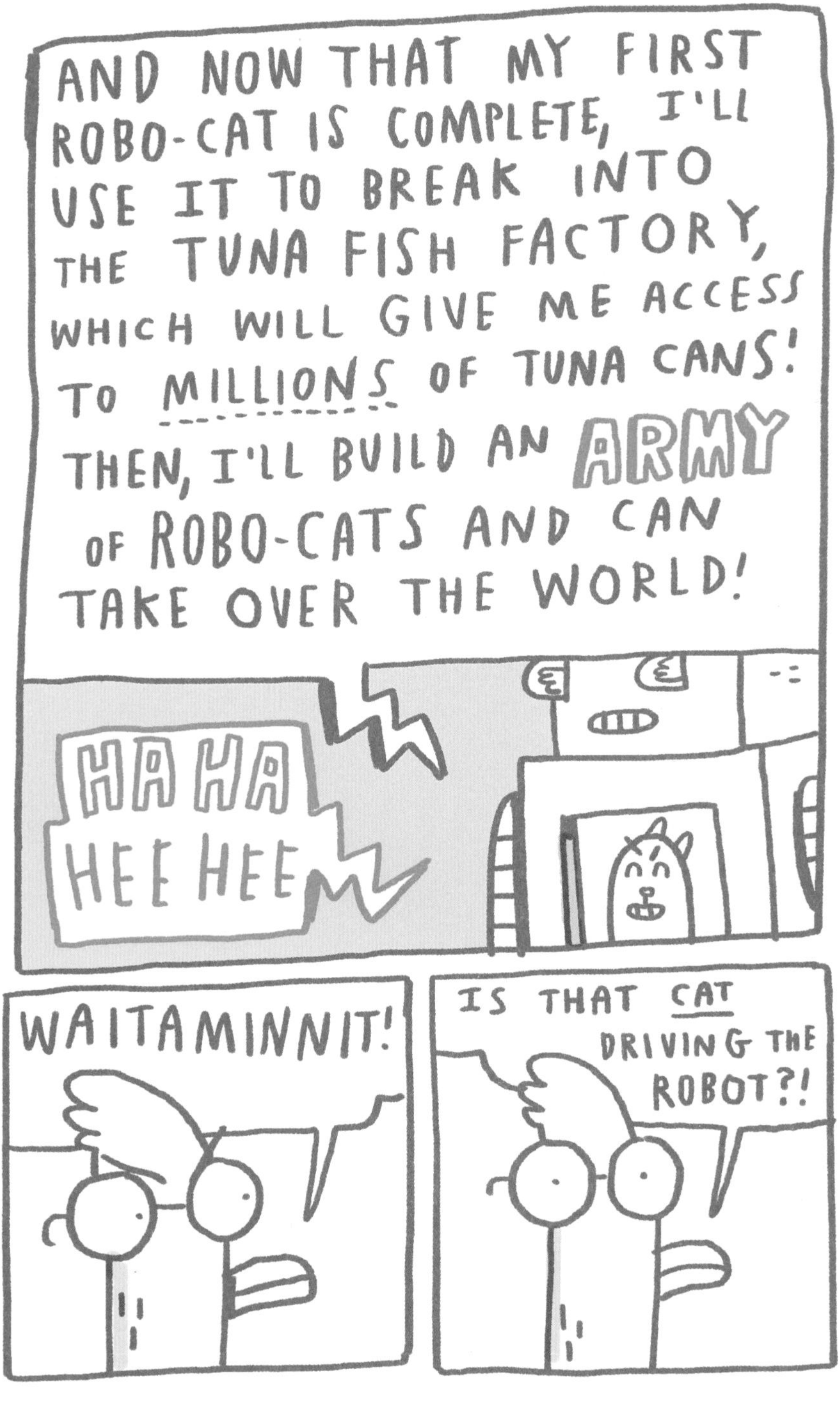
AND NOW THAT MY FIRST ROBO-CAT IS COMPLETE, I'LL USE IT TO BREAK INTO THE TUNA FISH FACTORY, WHICH WILL GIVE ME ACCESS TO MILLIONS OF TUNA CANS! THEN, I'LL BUILD AN ARMY OF ROBO-CATS AND CAN TAKE OVER THE WORLD!
HA HA HEE HEE
WAITAMINNIT!
IS THAT CAT DRIVING THE ROBOT?!

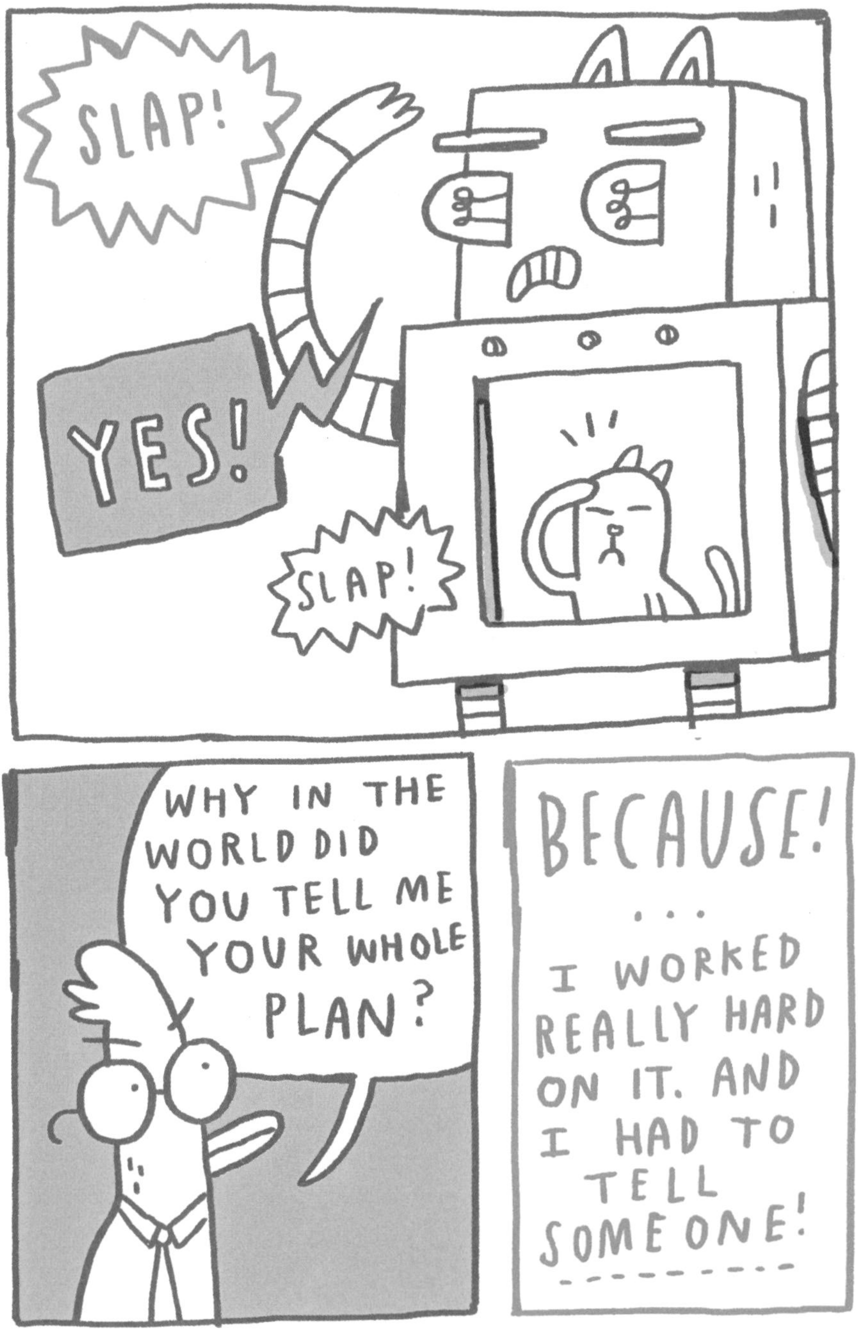
SLAP!
YES!
SLAP!
WHY IN THE WORLD DID YOU TELL ME YOUR WHOLE PLAN?
BECAUSE!
...
I WORKED REALLY HARD ON IT. AND I HAD TO TELL SOMEONE!

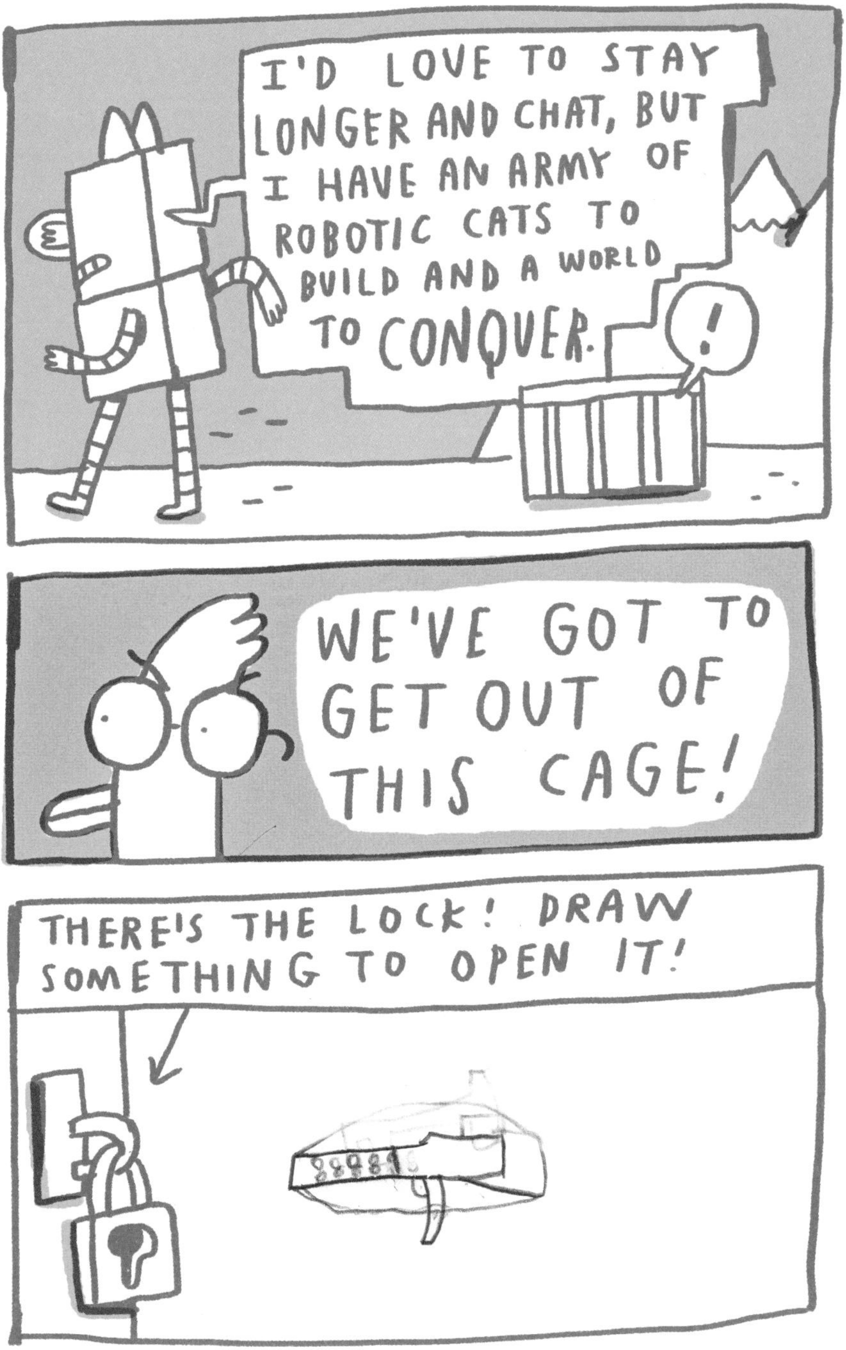
I'D LOVE TO STAY LONGER AND CHAT, BUT I HAVE AN ARMY OF ROBOTIC CATS TO BUILD AND A WORLD TO CONQUER.
!
WE'VE GOT TO GET OUT OF THIS CAGE!
THERE'S THE LOCK! DRAW SOMETHING TO OPEN IT!

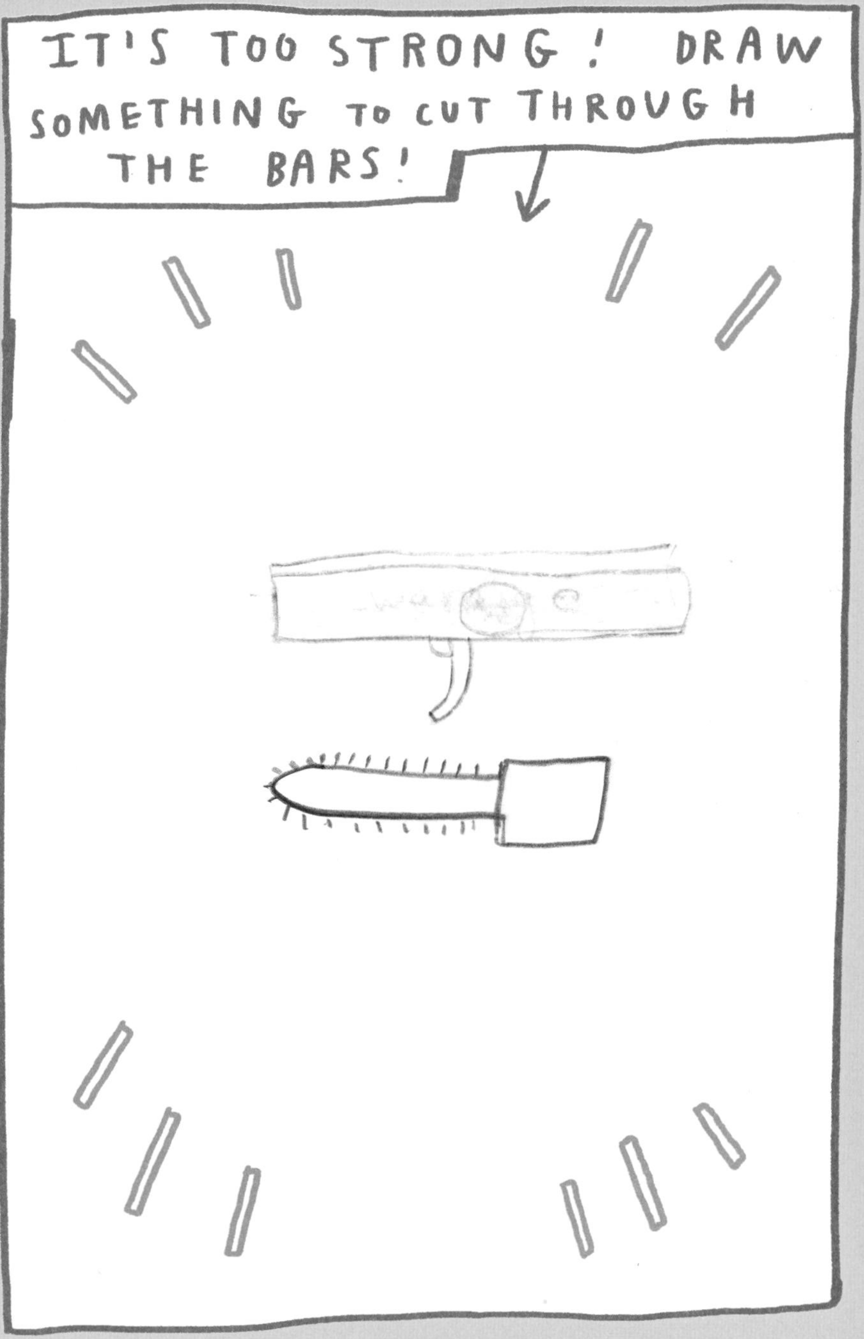
IT'S TOO STRONG! DRAW SOMETHING TO CUT THROUGH THE BARS!

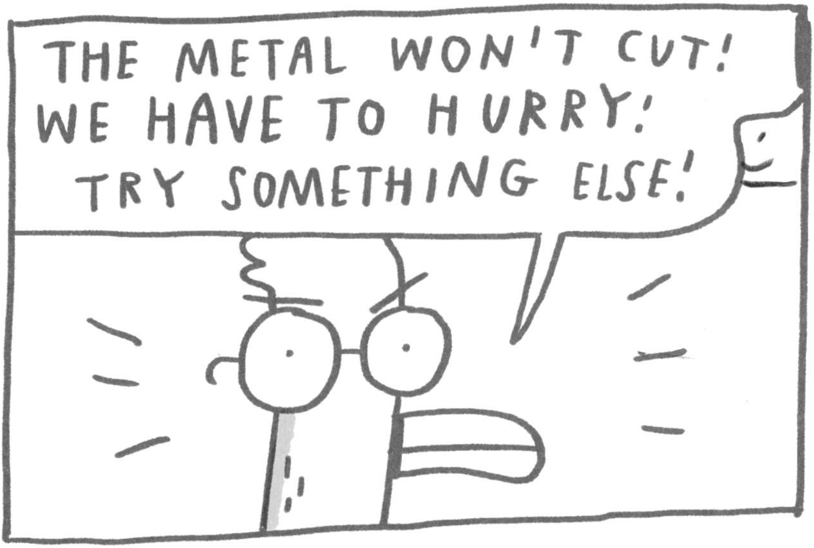
THE METAL WON'T CUT! WE HAVE TO HURRY! TRY SOMETHING ELSE!

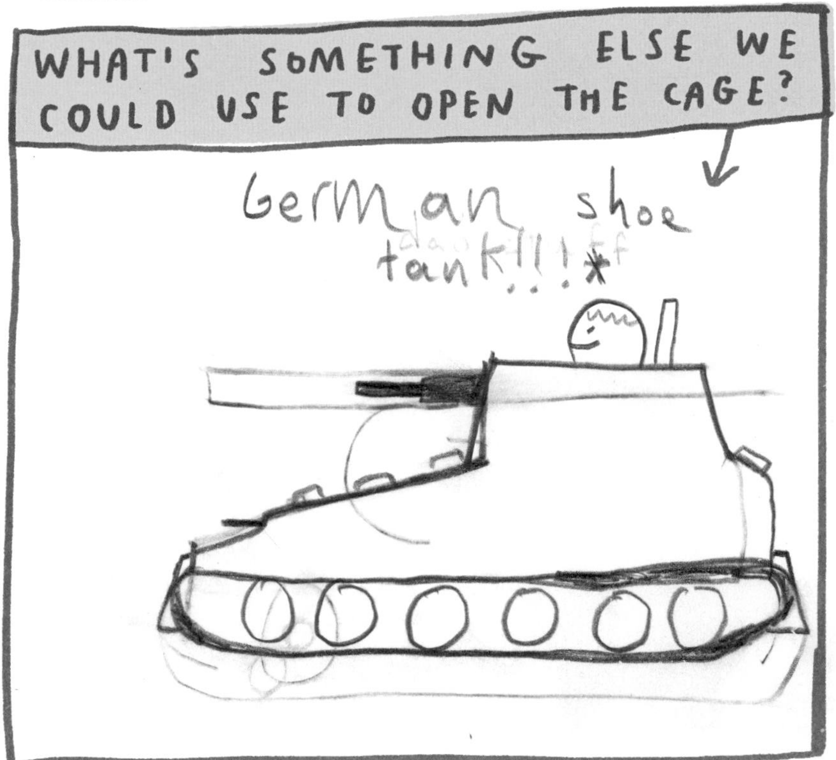
WHAT'S SOMETHING ELSE WE COULD USE TO OPEN THE CAGE?
German shoe
tank!!!*

* plus dad stuff

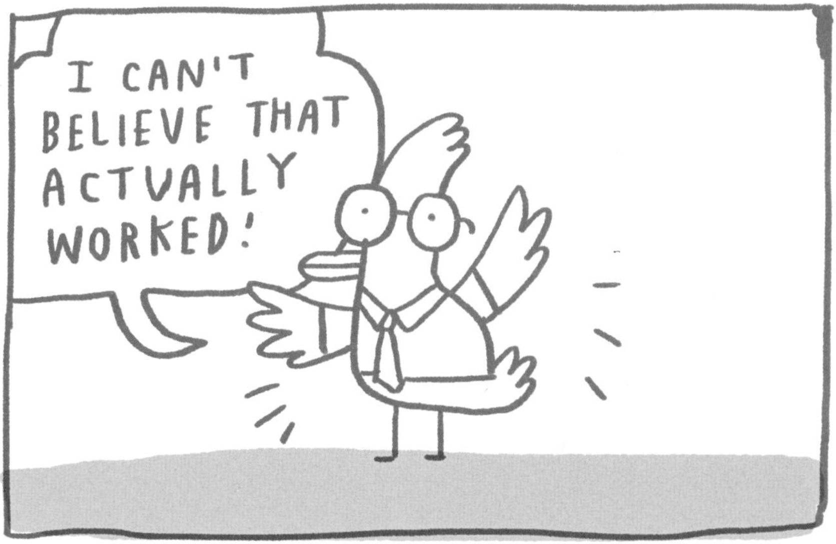
I CAN'T BELIEVE THAT ACTUALLY WORKED!

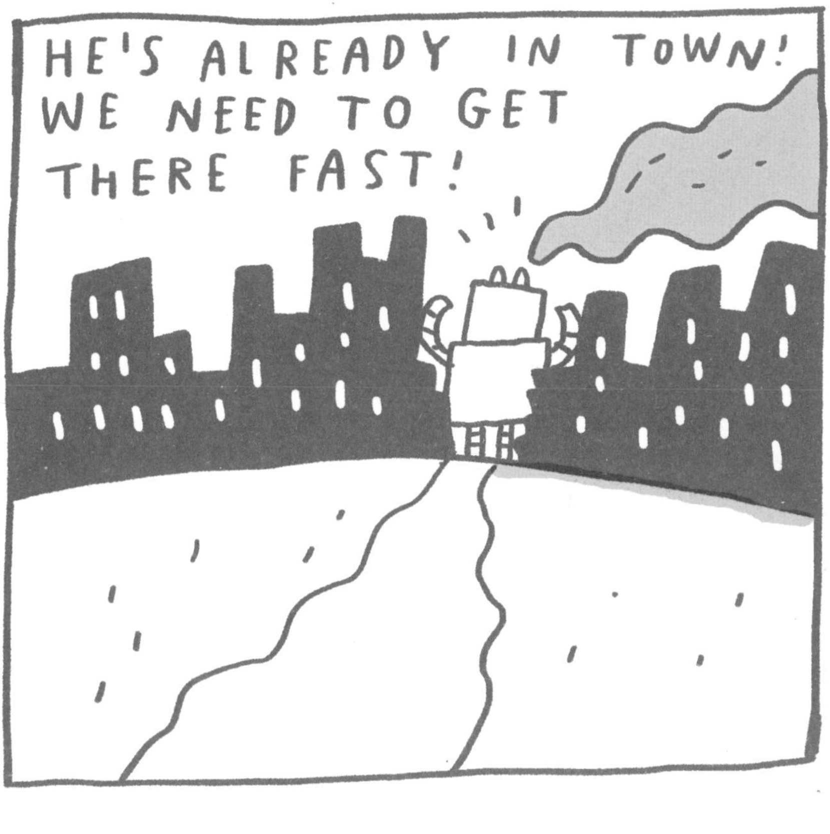
HE'S ALREADY IN TOWN! WE NEED TO GET THERE FAST!

DRAW A MACHINE THAT CAN GET US THERE **FAST!**

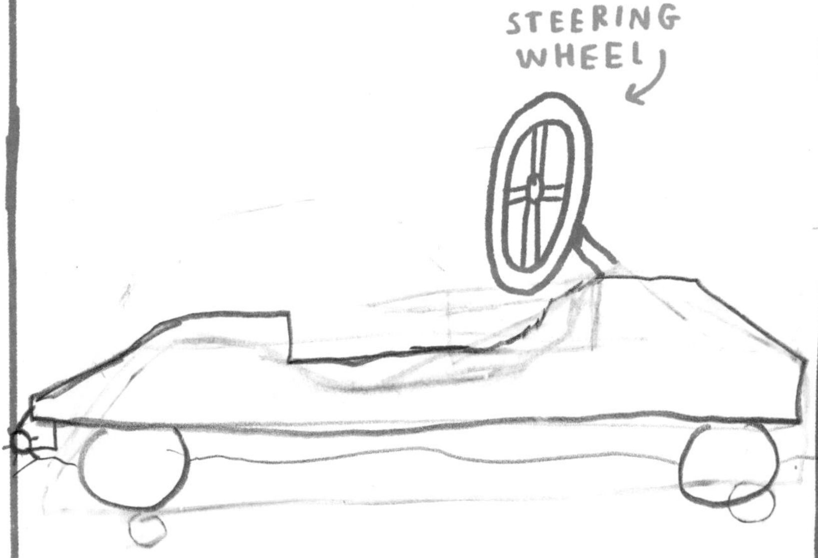
STEERING WHEEL

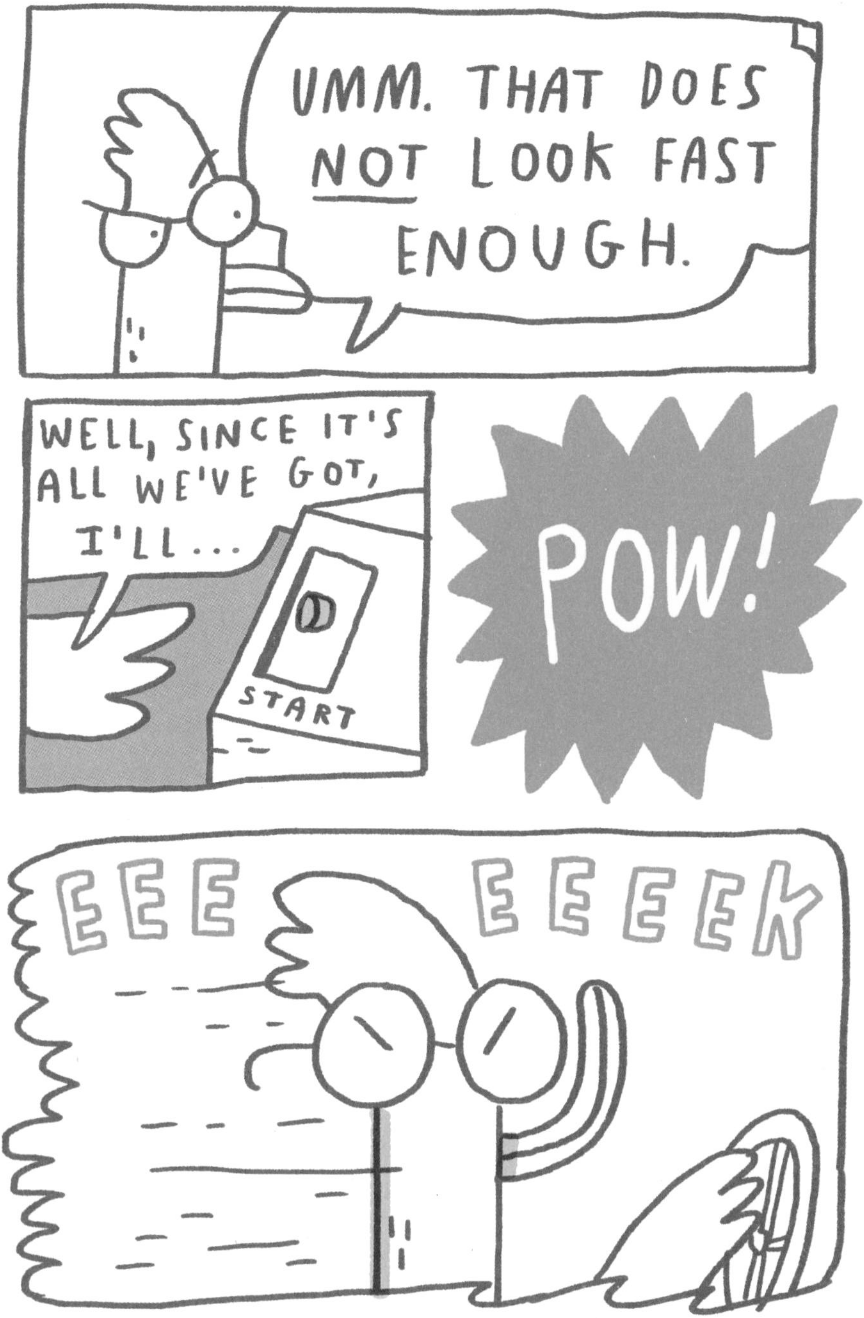
UMM. THAT DOES NOT LOOK FAST ENOUGH.
WELL, SINCE IT'S ALL WE'VE GOT, I'LL...
START
POW!
EEE EEEEK

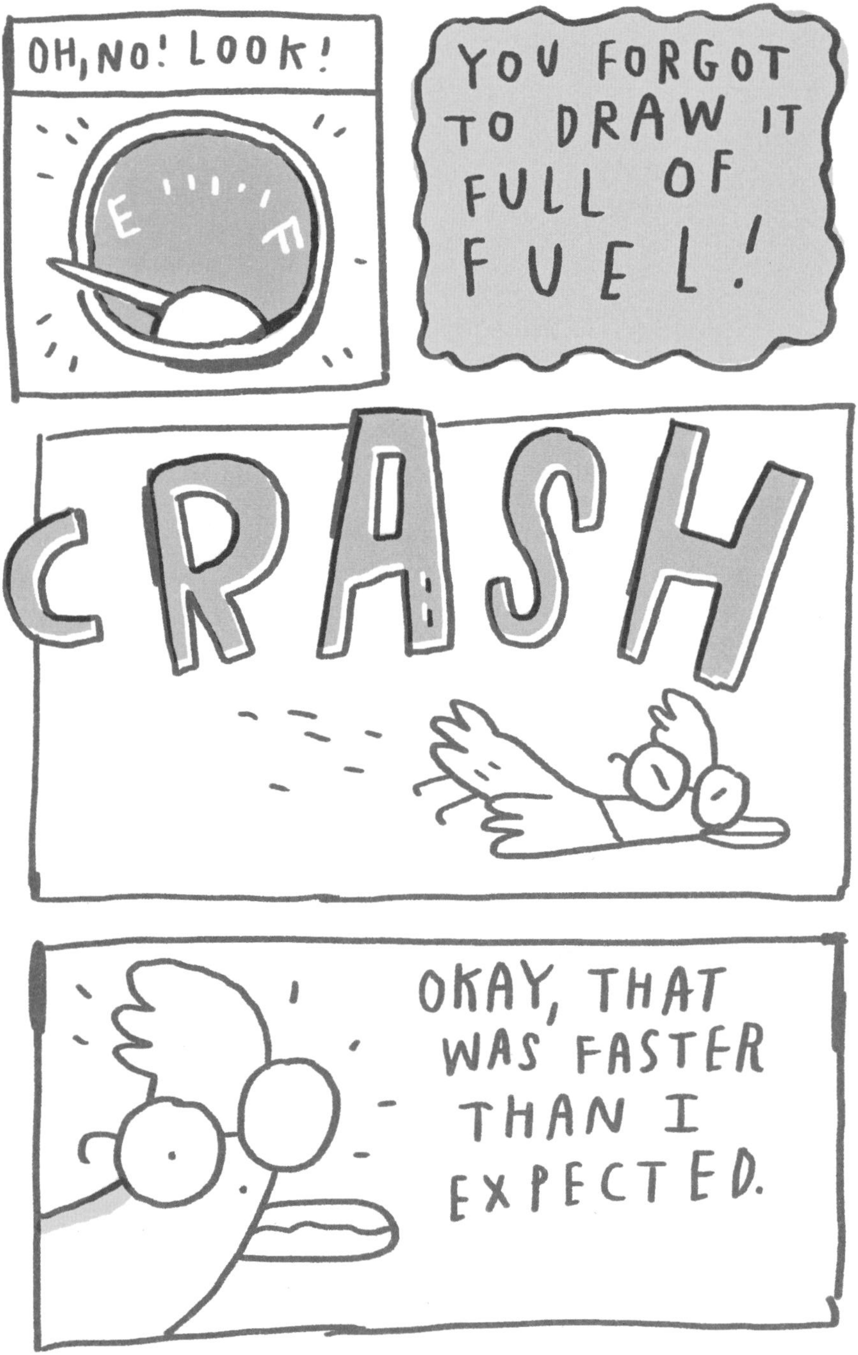
OH, NO! LOOK!
E
F
YOU FORGOT TO DRAW IT FULL OF FUEL!
CRASH
OKAY, THAT WAS FASTER THAN I EXPECTED.

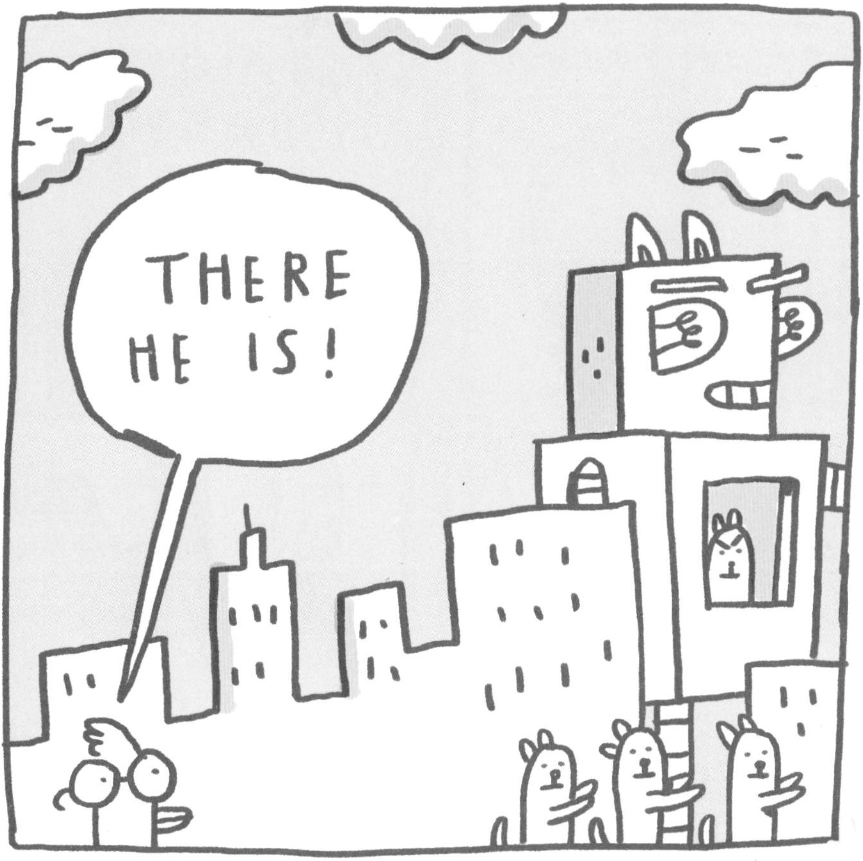
THERE HE IS!

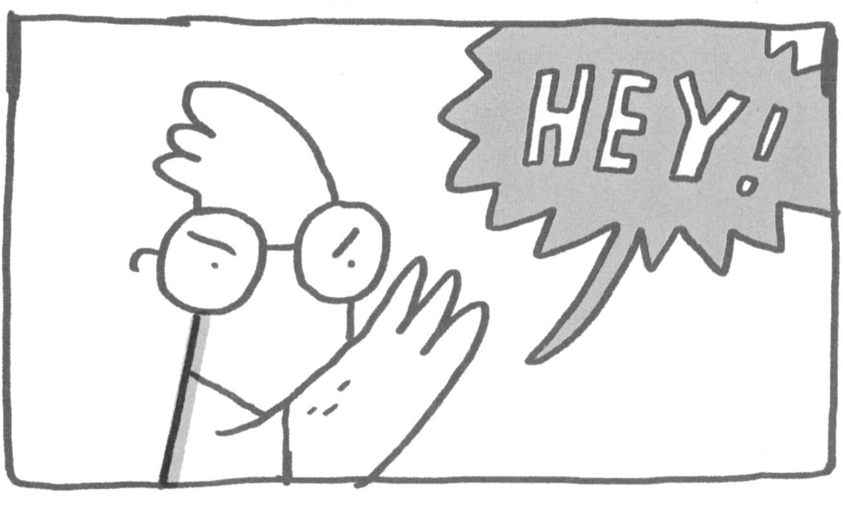
HEY!

HE CAN'T HEAR US! DRAW SOMETHING **LOUD** to GET HIS ATTENTION!

my older brother
Who I
really like
see
trumpet

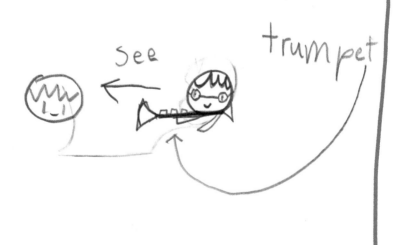

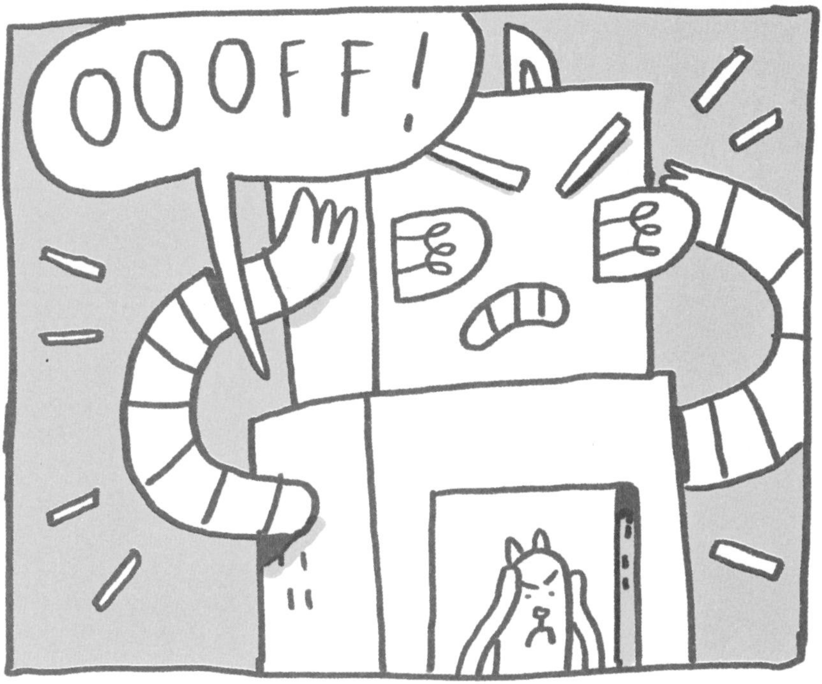
OOOFF!

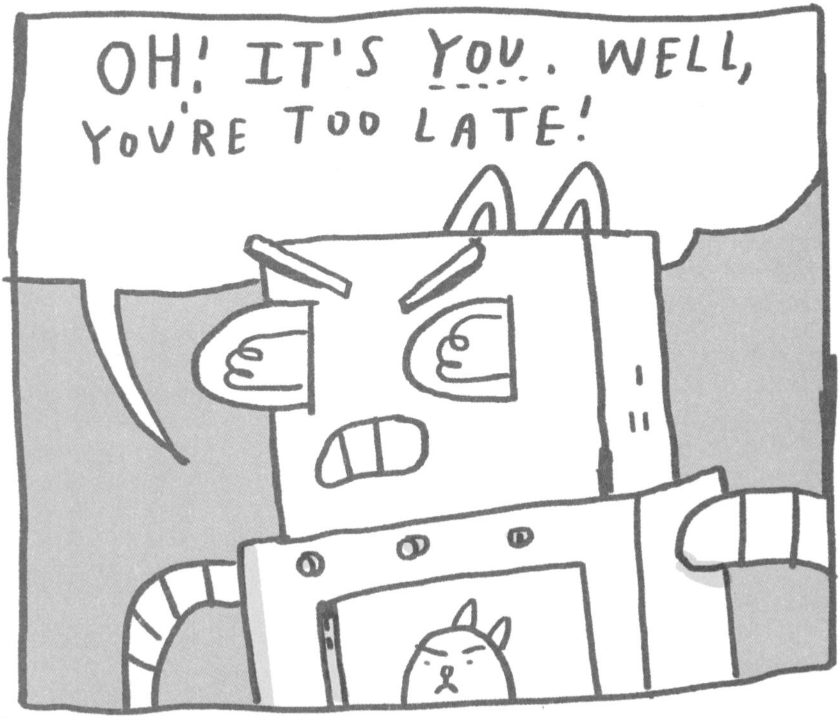
OH! IT'S YOU. WELL, YOU'RE TOO LATE!

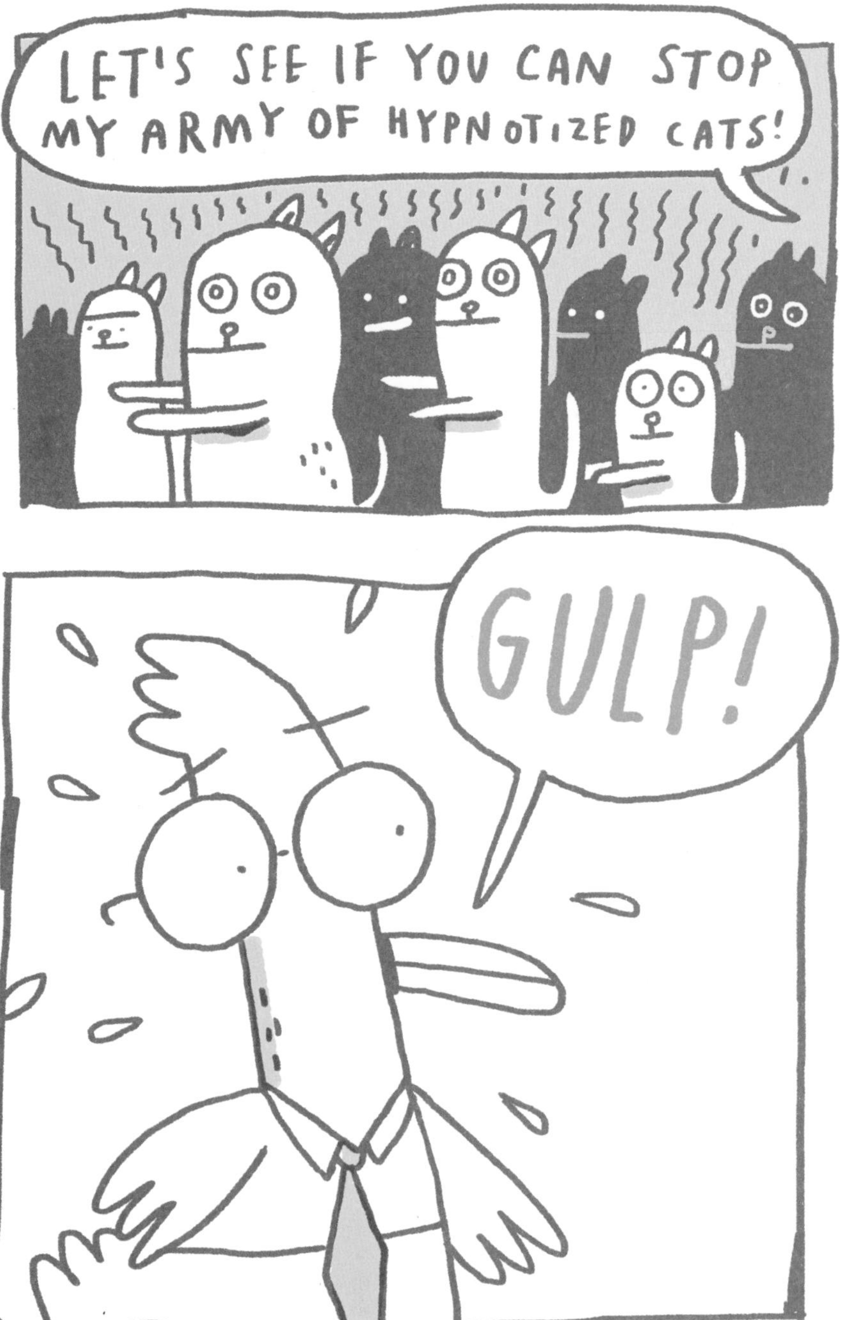
LET'S SEE IF YOU CAN STOP MY ARMY OF HYPNOTIZED CATS!
GULP!

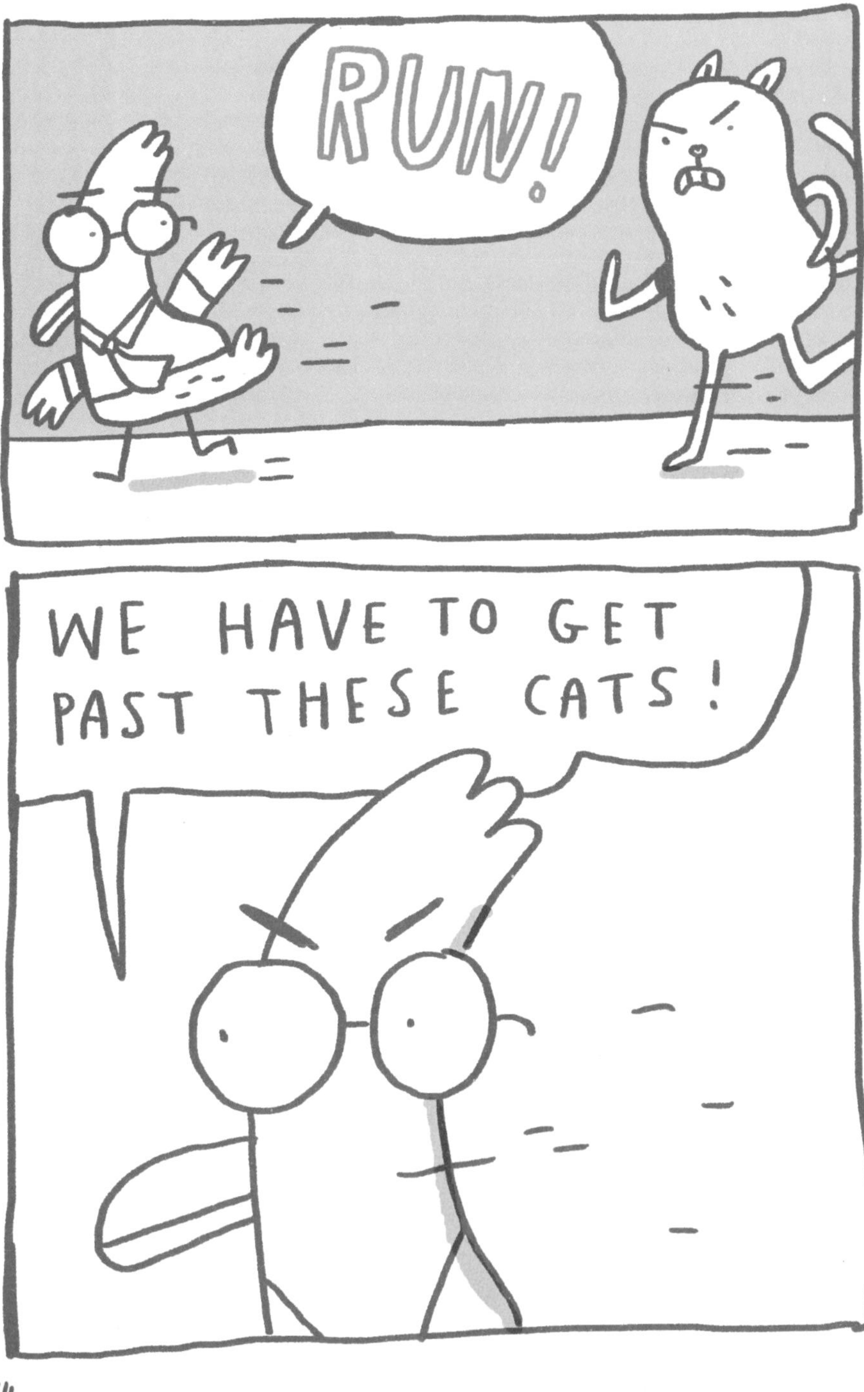
RUN!
WE HAVE TO GET PAST THESE CATS!

DRAW A GIANT ANGRY DOG TO SCARE THEM AWAY!

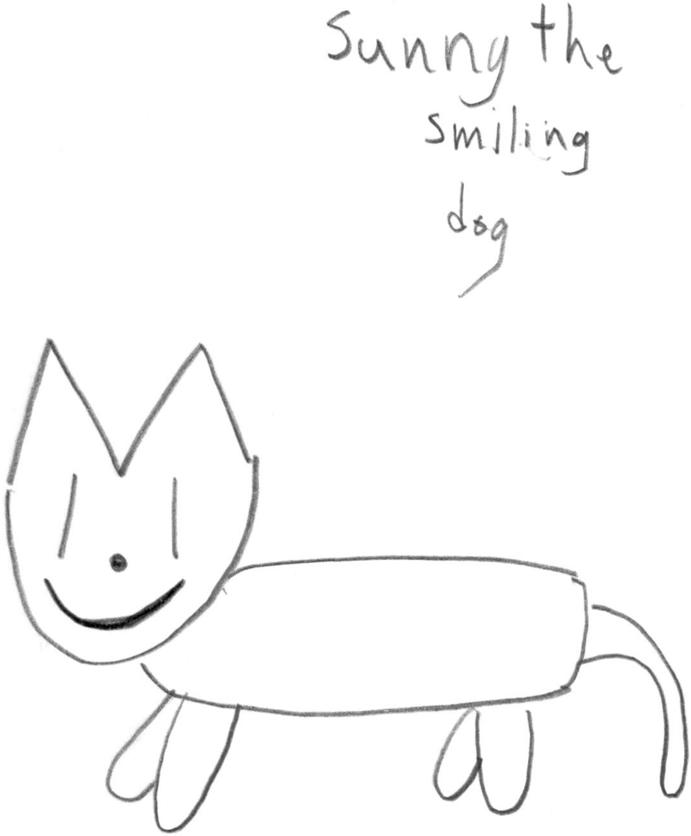
Sunny the smiling dog

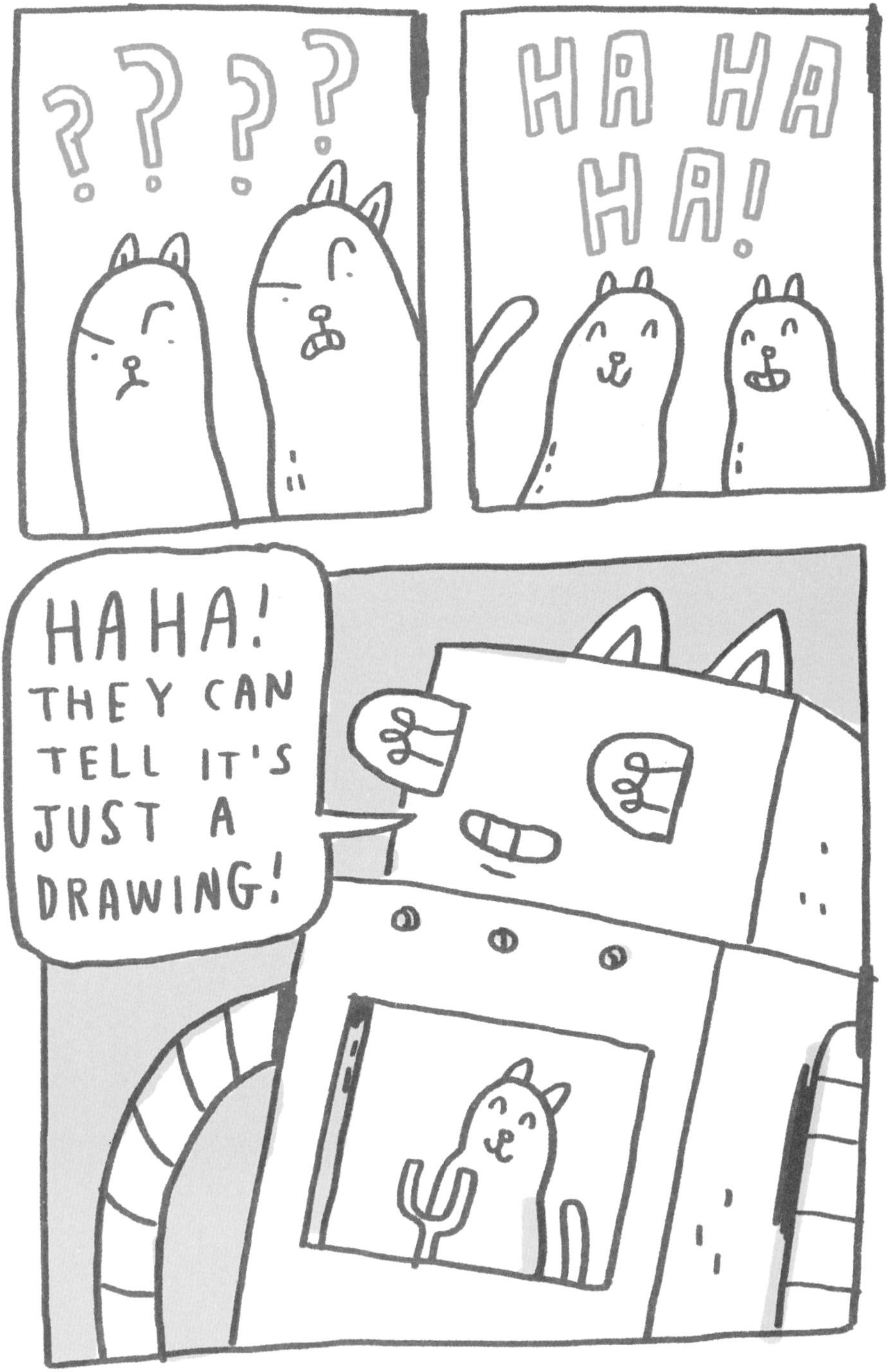
? ? ? ?
HA HA HA HA!
HAHA! THEY CAN TELL IT'S JUST A DRAWING!

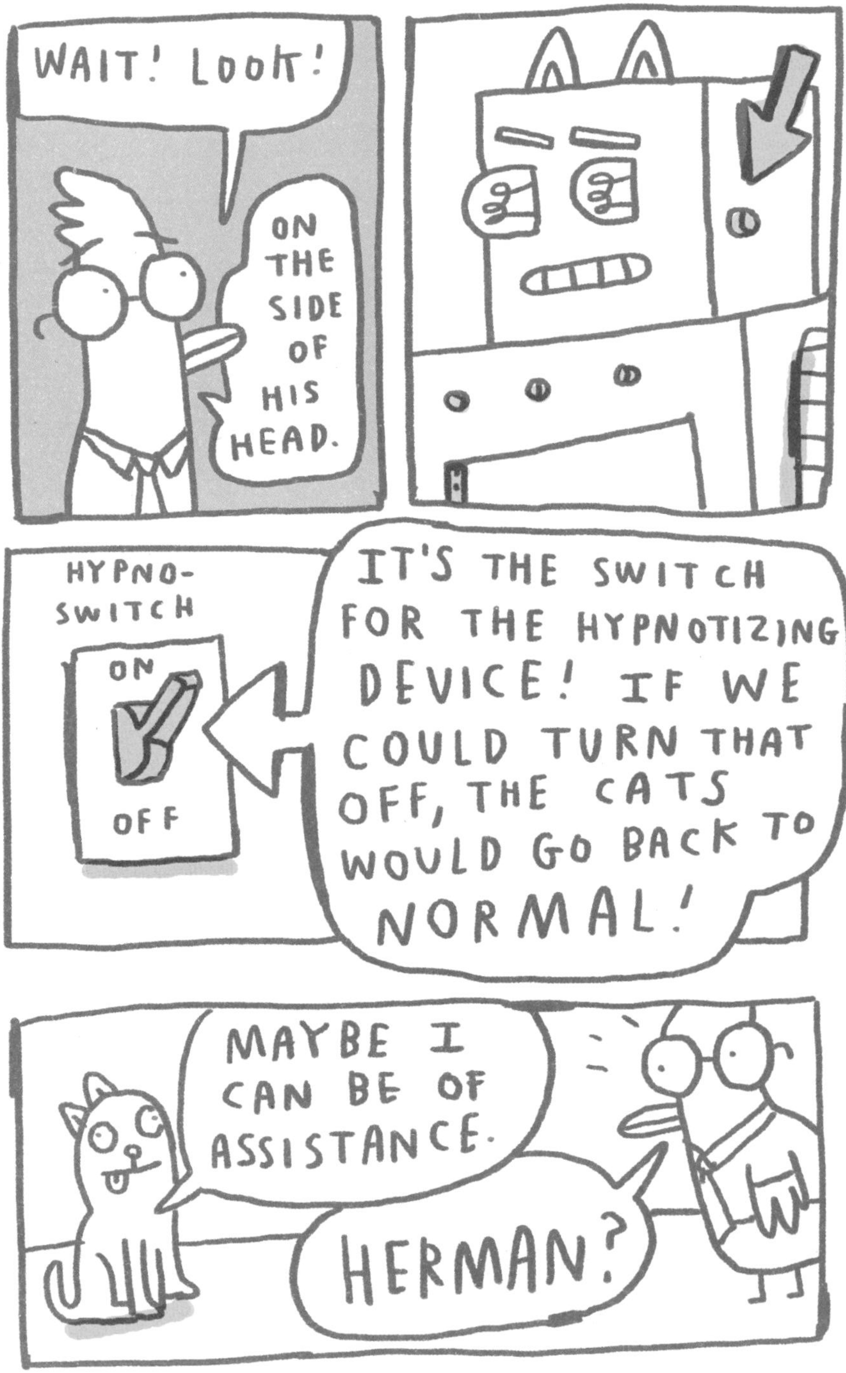

WAIT! LOOK!
ON THE SIDE OF HIS HEAD.
HYPNO-SWITCH
ON
OFF
IT'S THE SWITCH FOR THE HYPNOTIZING DEVICE! IF WE COULD TURN THAT OFF, THE CATS WOULD GO BACK TO NORMAL!
MAYBE I CAN BE OF ASSISTANCE.
HERMAN?

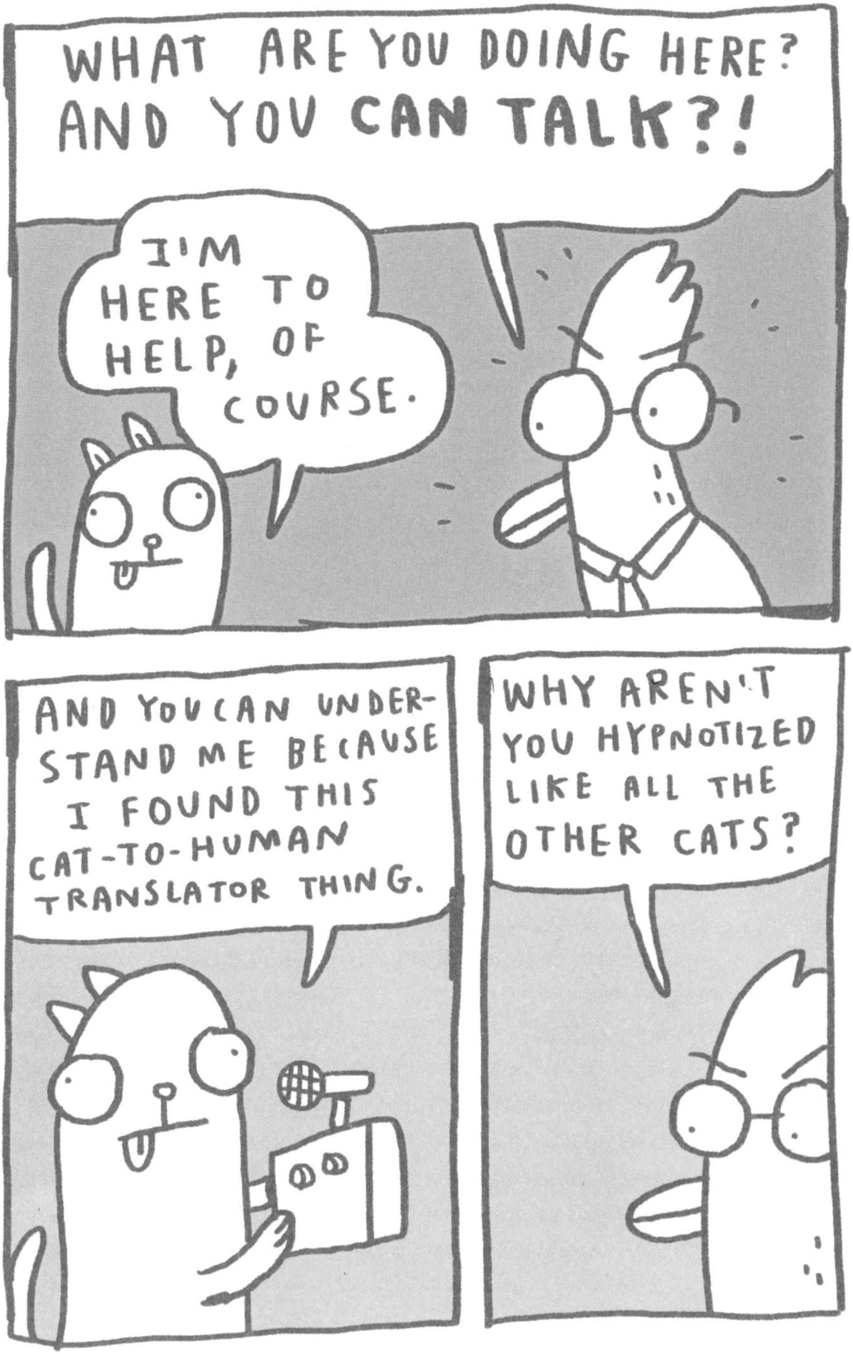
WHAT ARE YOU DOING HERE? AND YOU CAN TALK?!
I'M HERE TO HELP, OF COURSE.
AND YOU CAN UNDERSTAND ME BECAUSE I FOUND THIS CAT-TO-HUMAN TRANSLATOR THING.
WHY AREN'T YOU HYPNOTIZED LIKE ALL THE OTHER CATS?

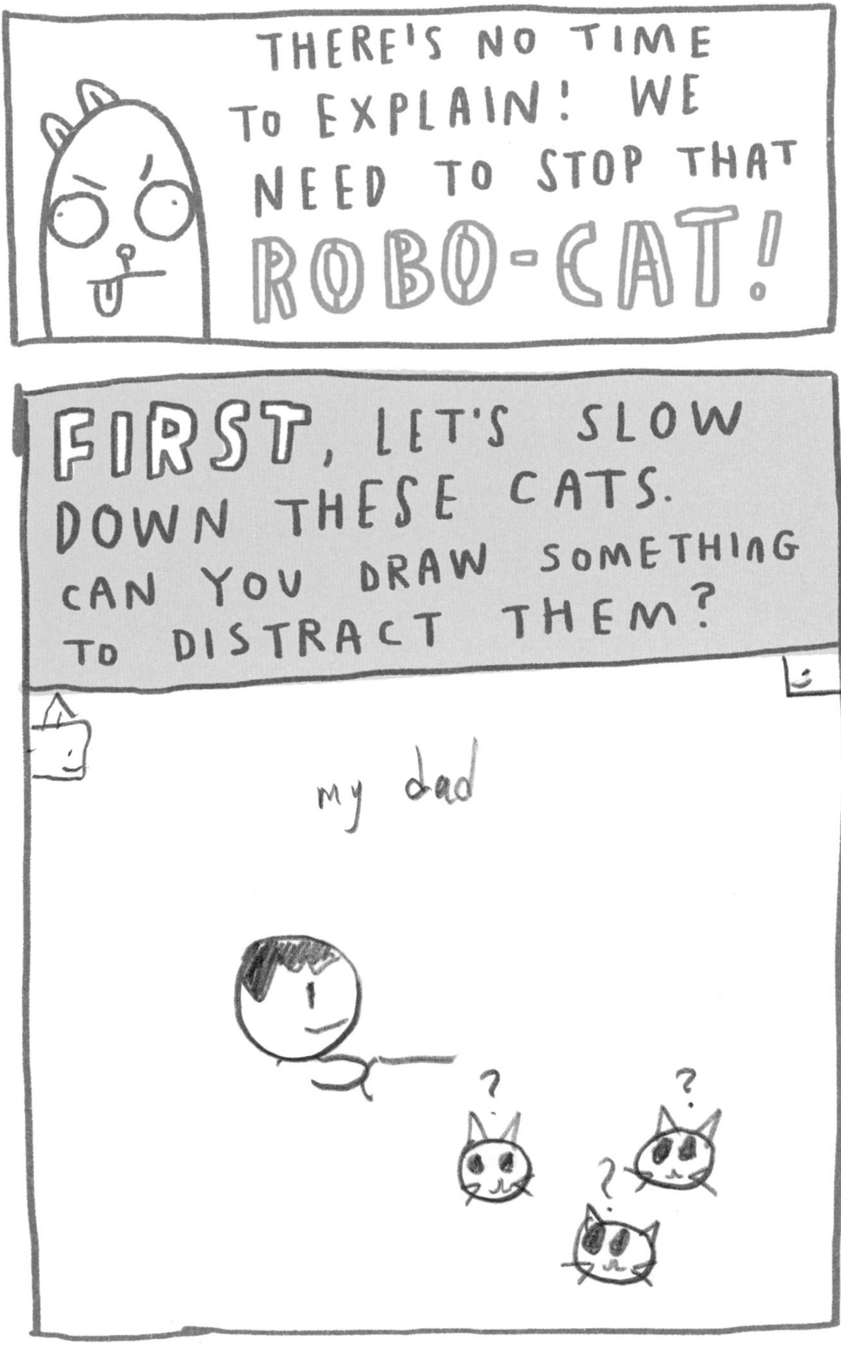
THERE'S NO TIME TO EXPLAIN! WE NEED TO STOP THAT ROBO-CAT!
FIRST, LET'S SLOW DOWN THESE CATS. CAN YOU DRAW SOMETHING TO DISTRACT THEM?
my dad
?
?
?

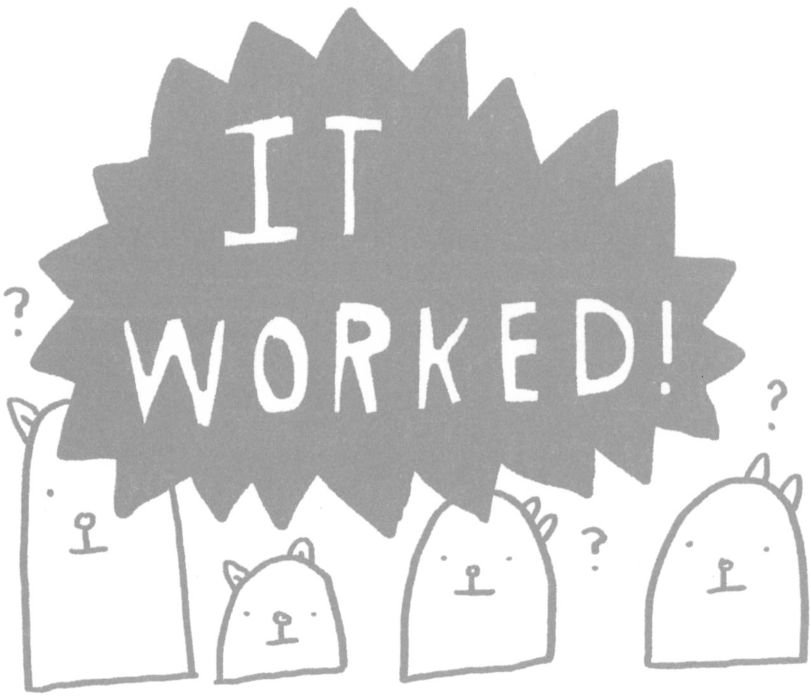
IT WORKED!
?
?
?

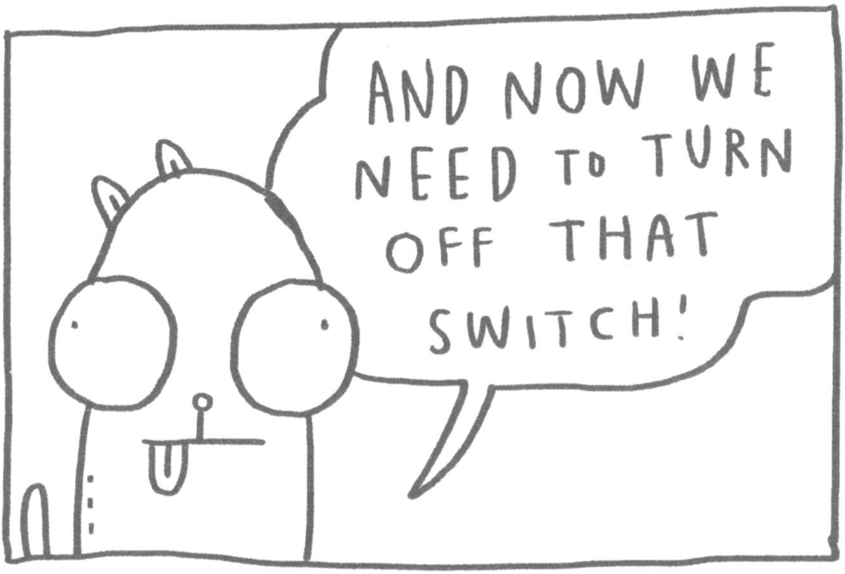
AND NOW WE NEED TO TURN OFF THAT SWITCH!

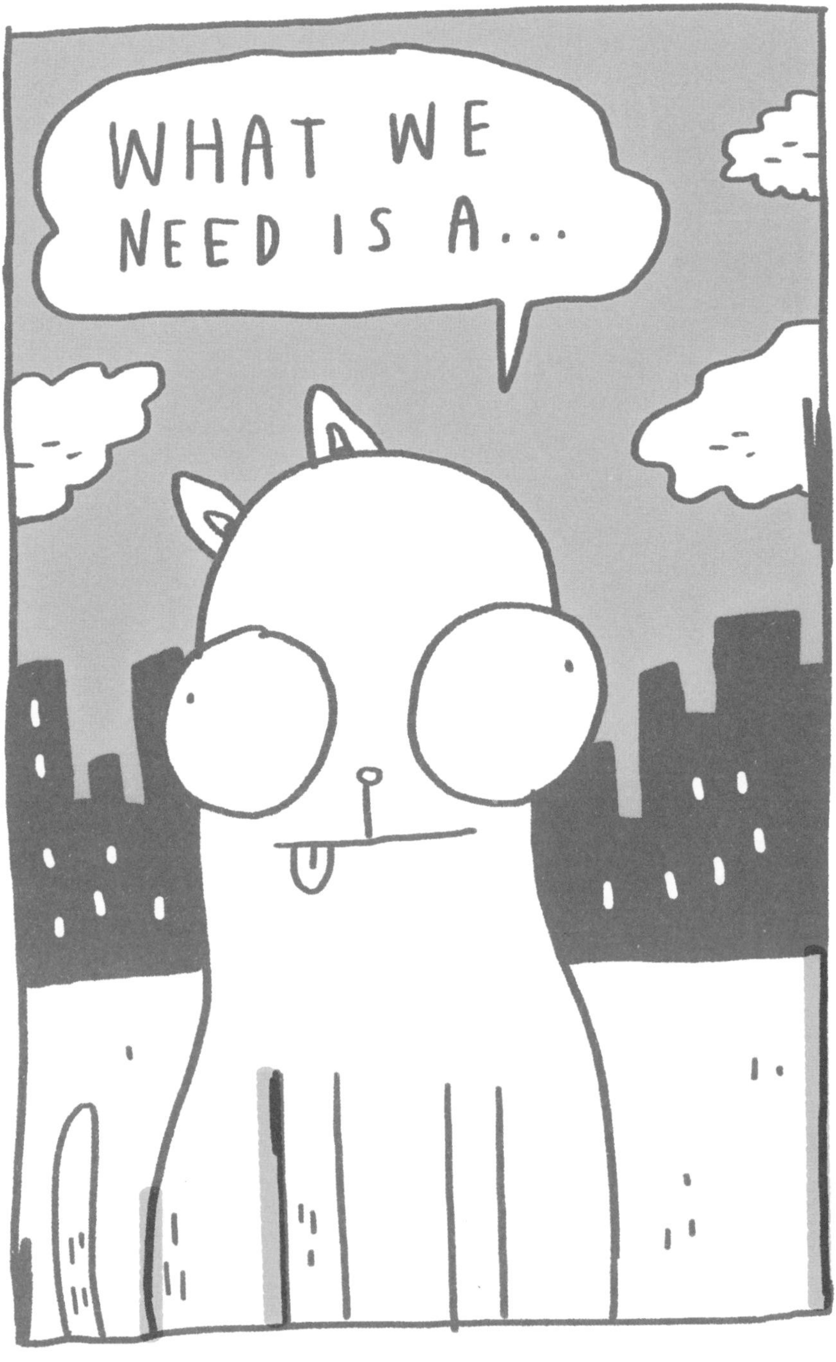
WHAT WE NEED IS A...

CAT-A-PULT!

DRAW SOMETHING TO LAUNCH HERMAN UP TO TURN OFF THE SWITCH!

I GOT THIS!

this
push
that

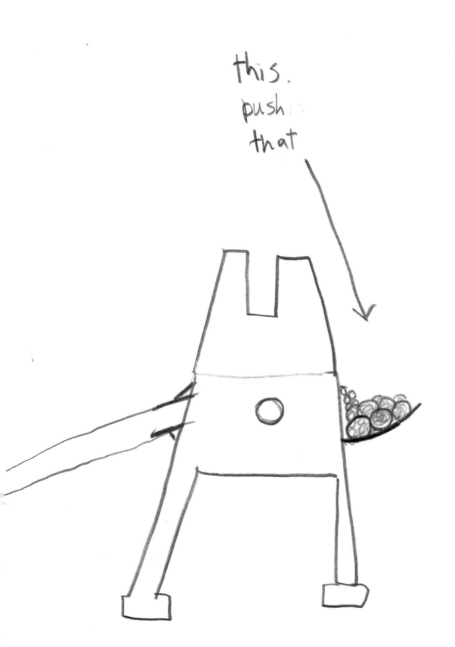

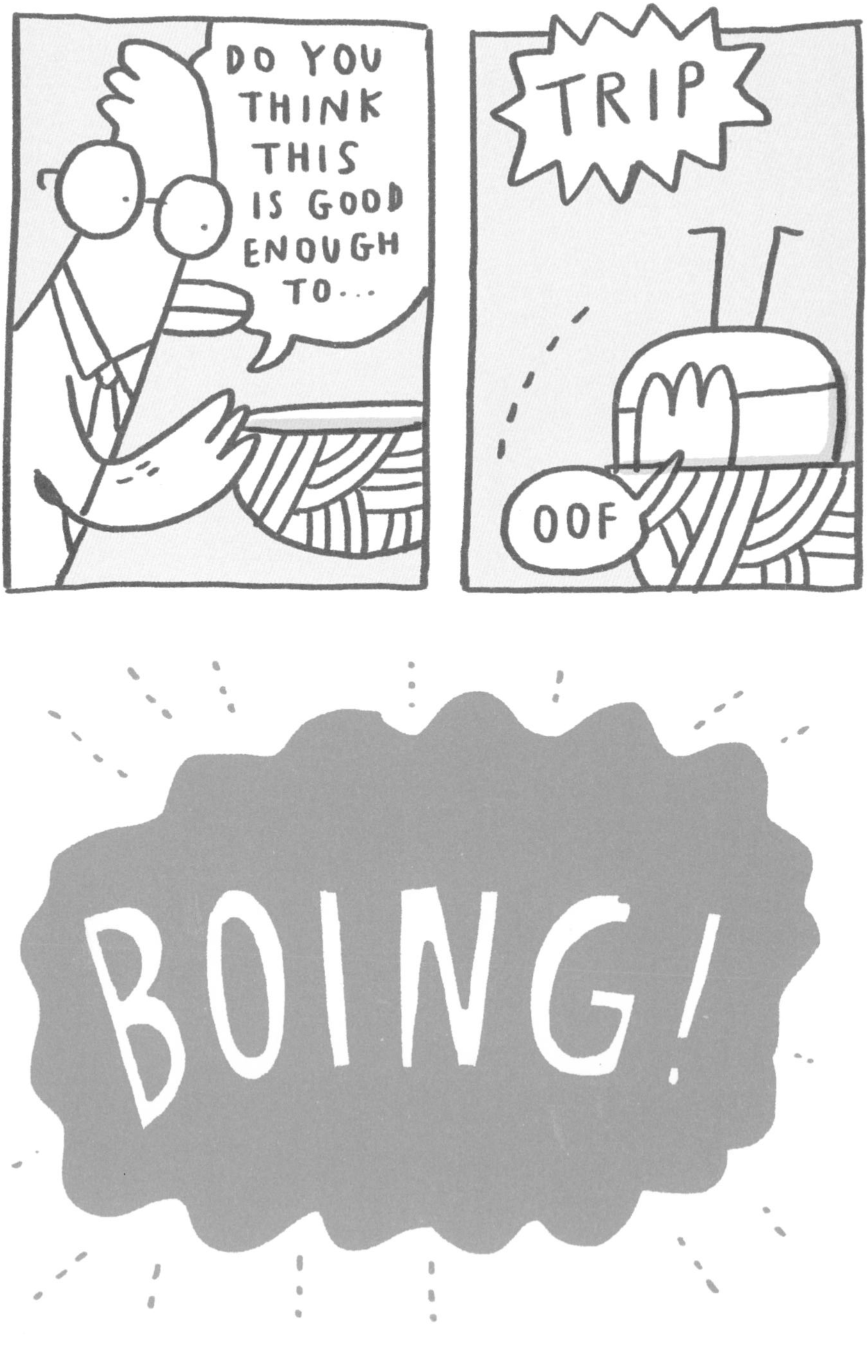
DO YOU THINK THIS IS GOOD ENOUGH TO...
TRIP
OOF
BOING!

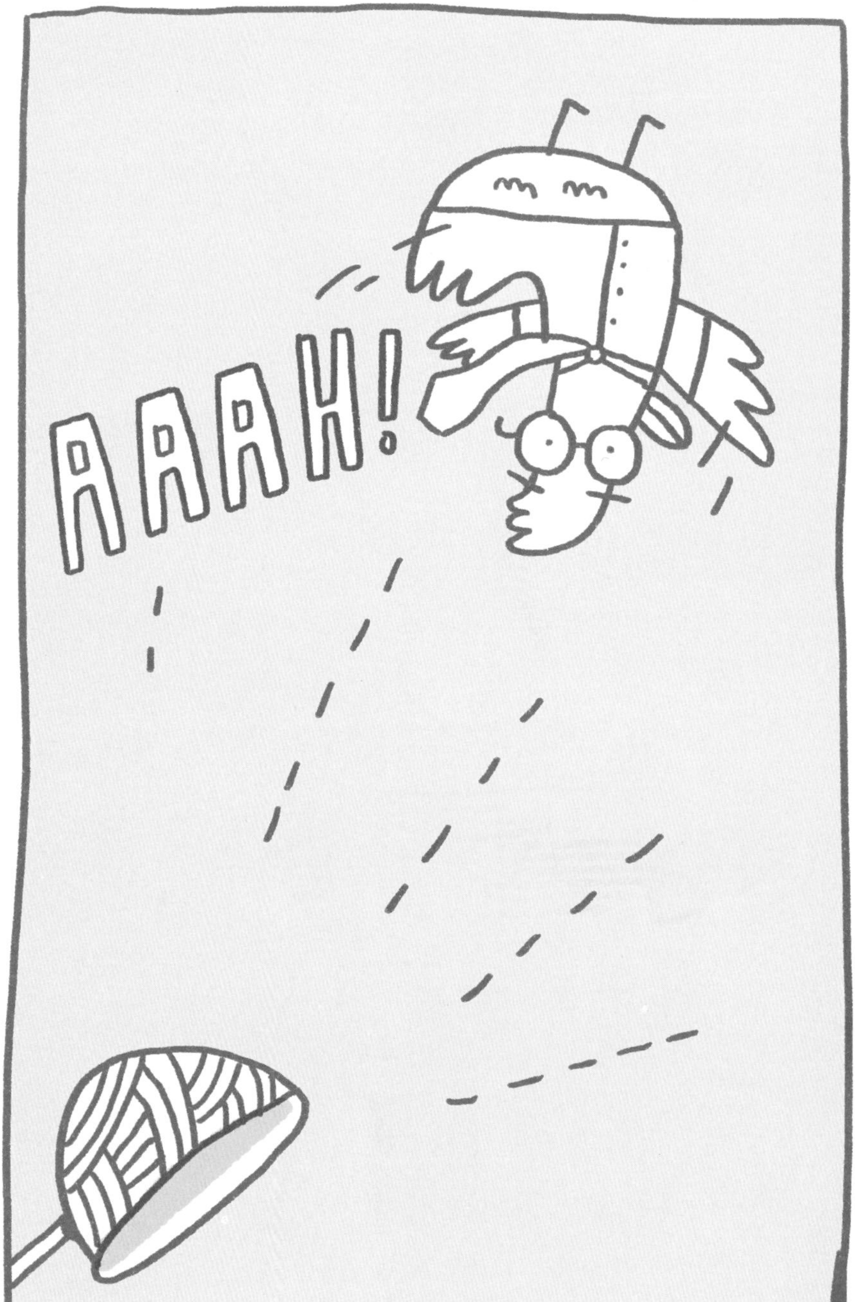
AAAH!

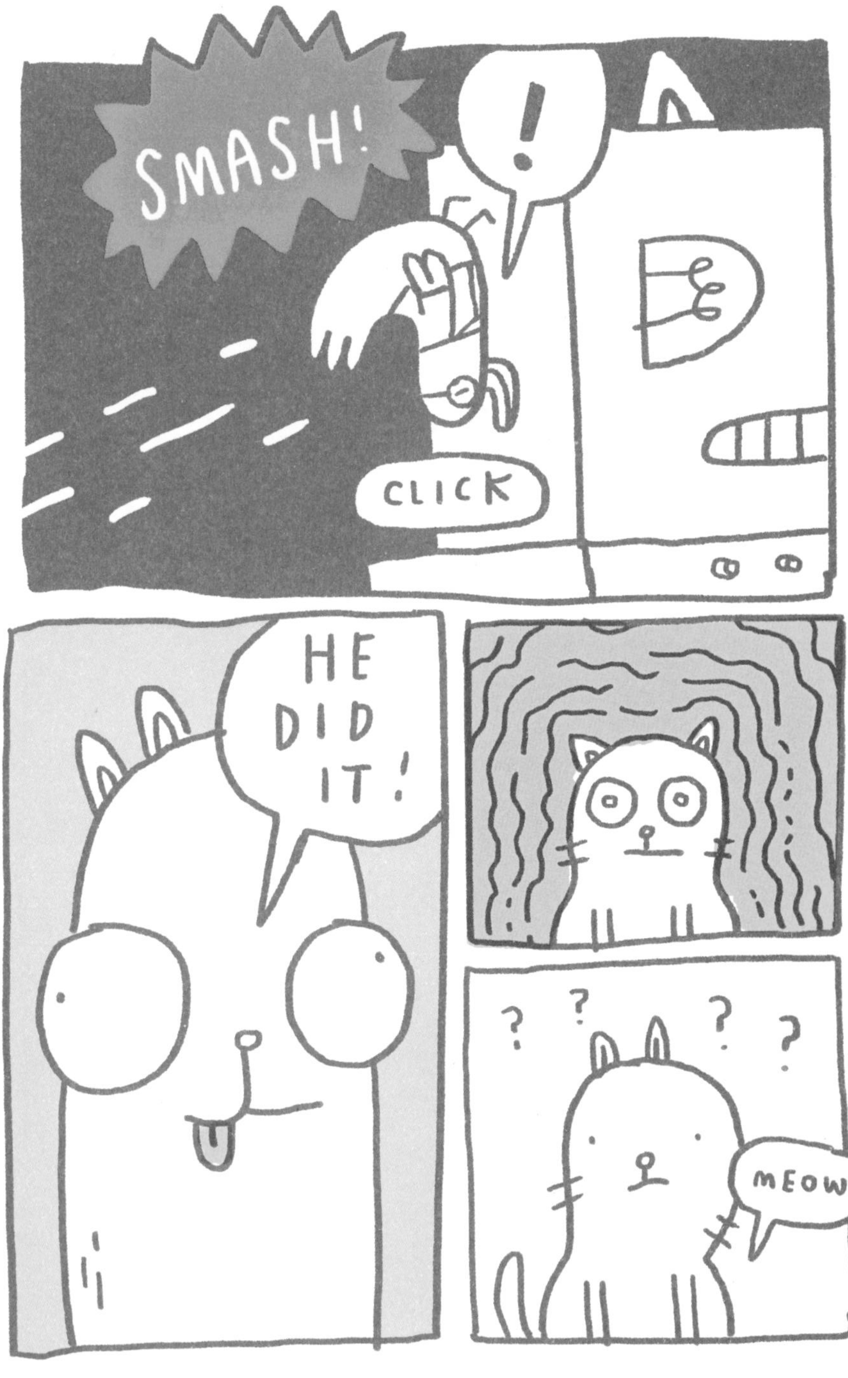
SMASH!
!
CLICK
HE DID IT!
? ? ? ?
MEOW

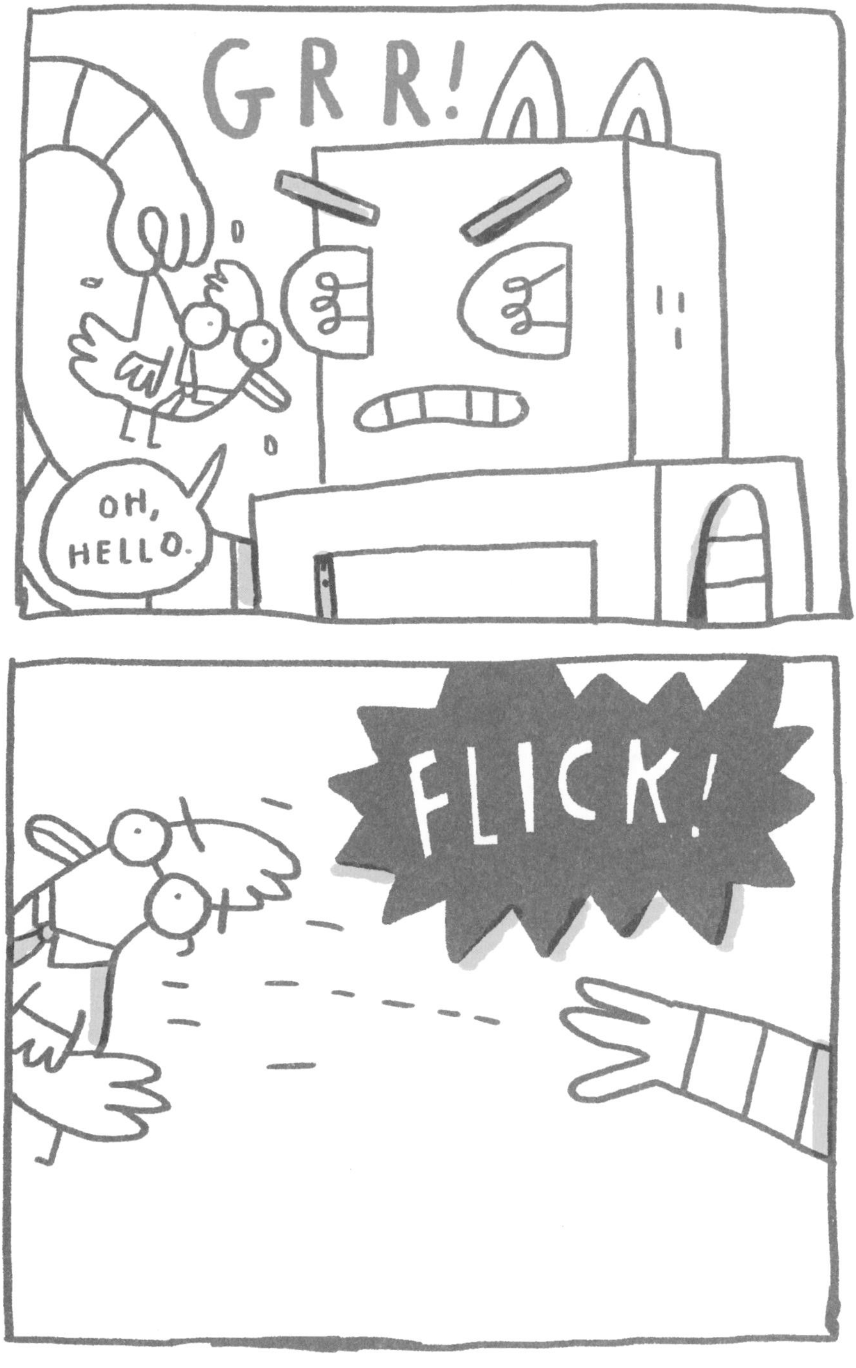
GRR!
OH, HELLO.
FLICK!

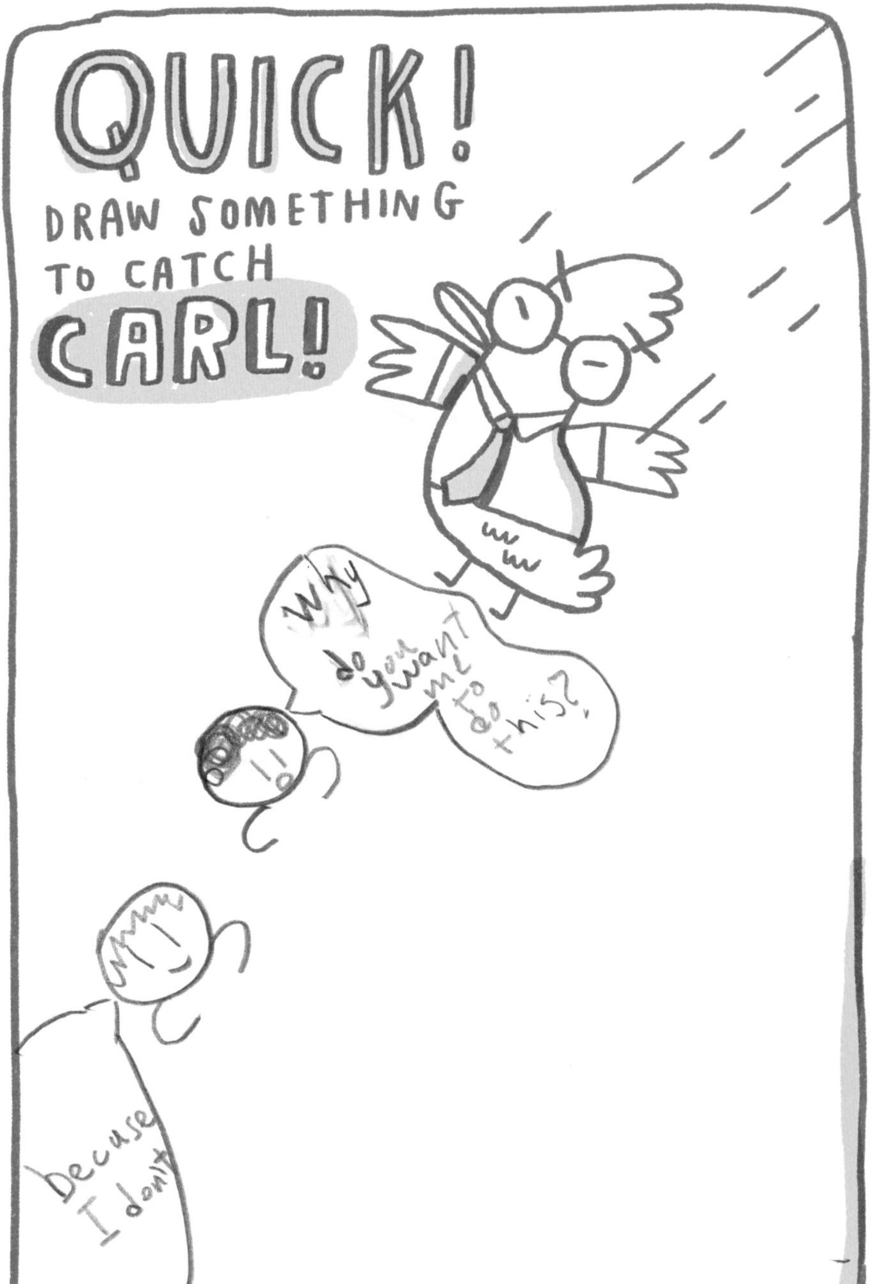
QUICK!
DRAW SOMETHING TO CATCH CARL!
Why do you want me to do this?
becuse I don't

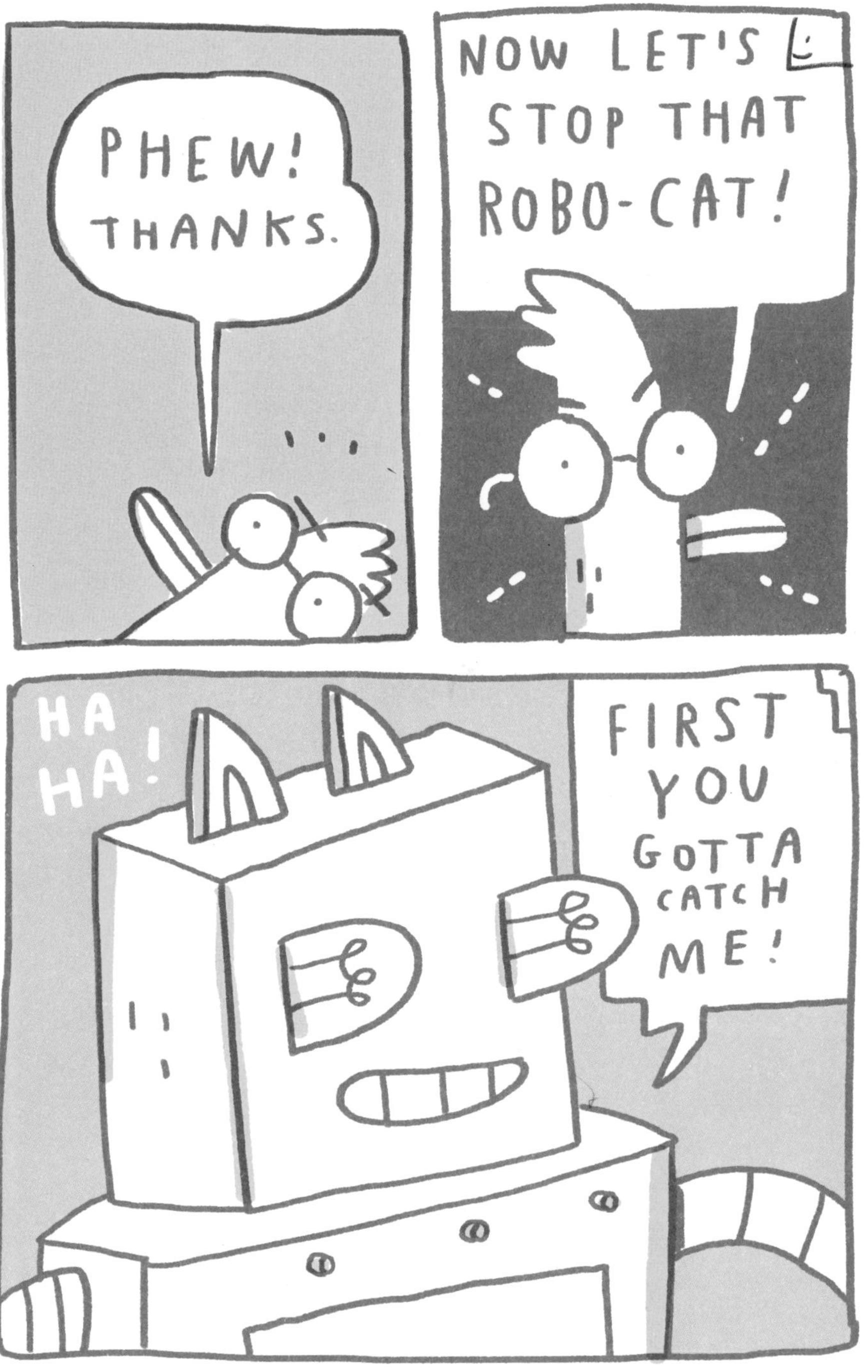
PHEW! THANKS.
NOW LET'S STOP THAT ROBO-CAT!
HA HA!
FIRST YOU GOTTA CATCH ME!

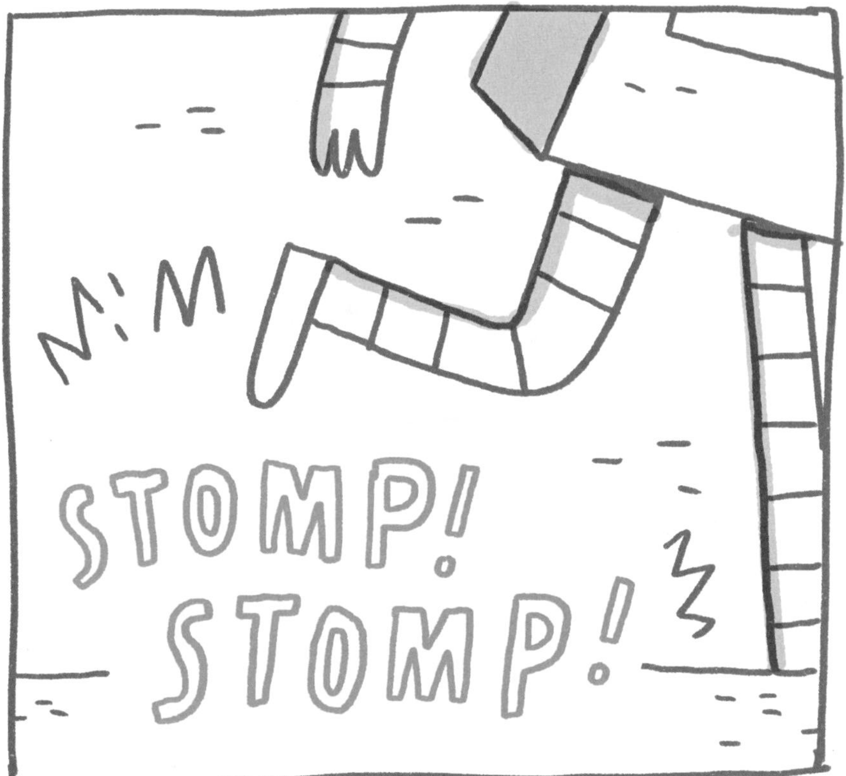
STOMP! STOMP!

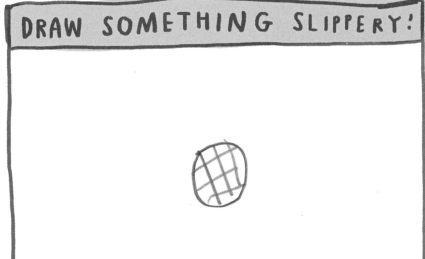

DRAW SOMETHING SLIPPERY!

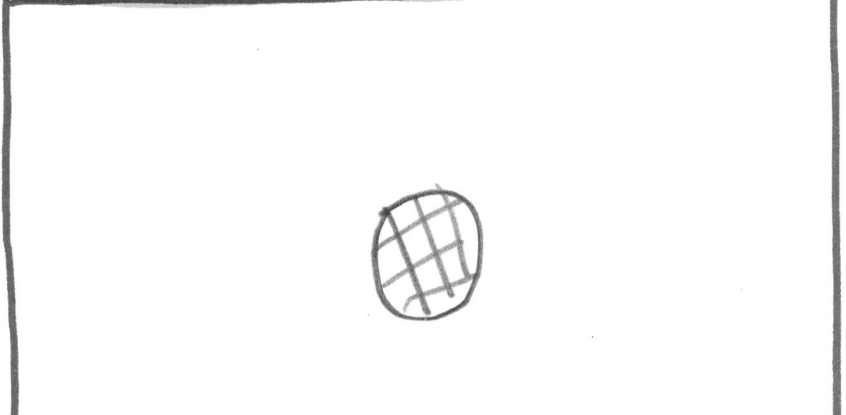

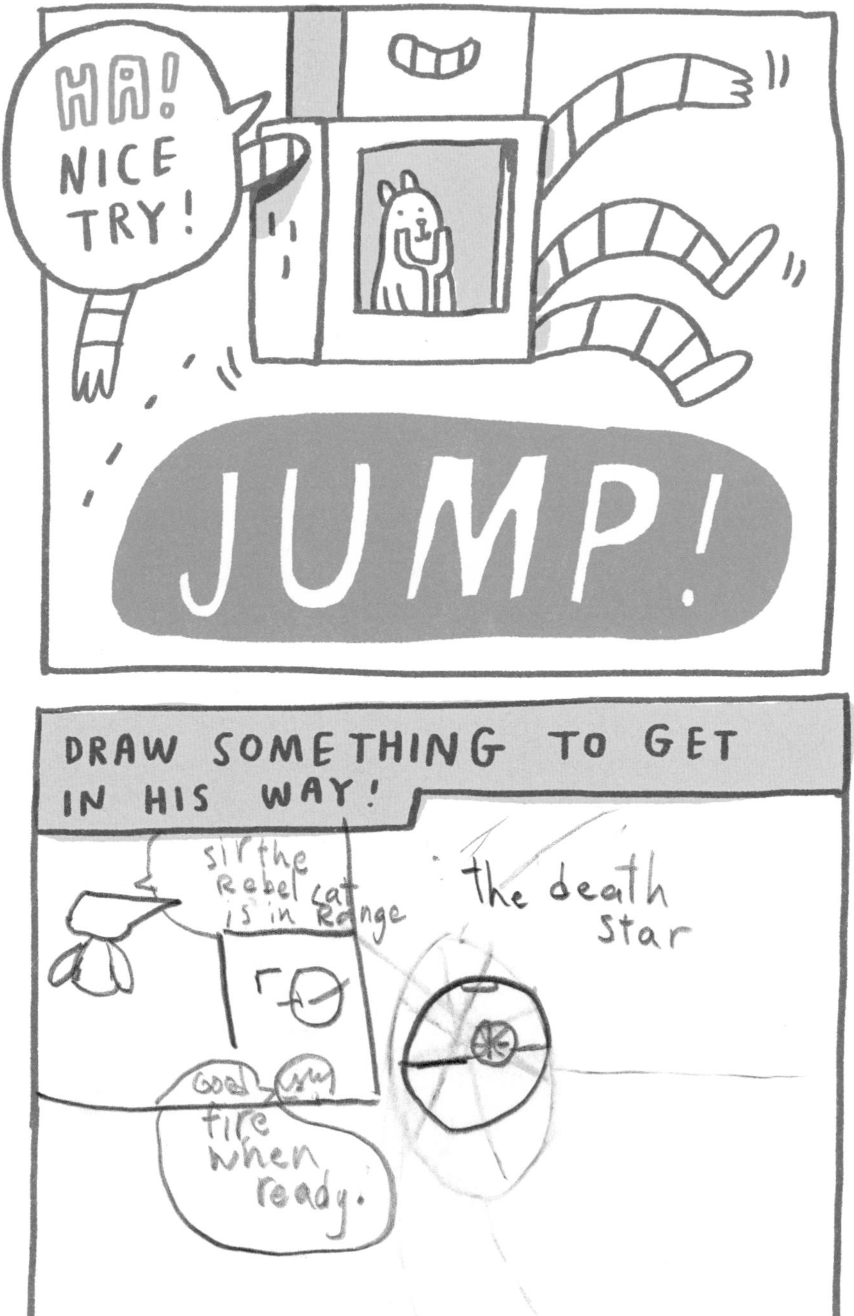
HA! NICE TRY!
JUMP!
DRAW SOMETHING TO GET IN HIS WAY!
sir the Rebel cat is in Range
the death star
fire when ready.

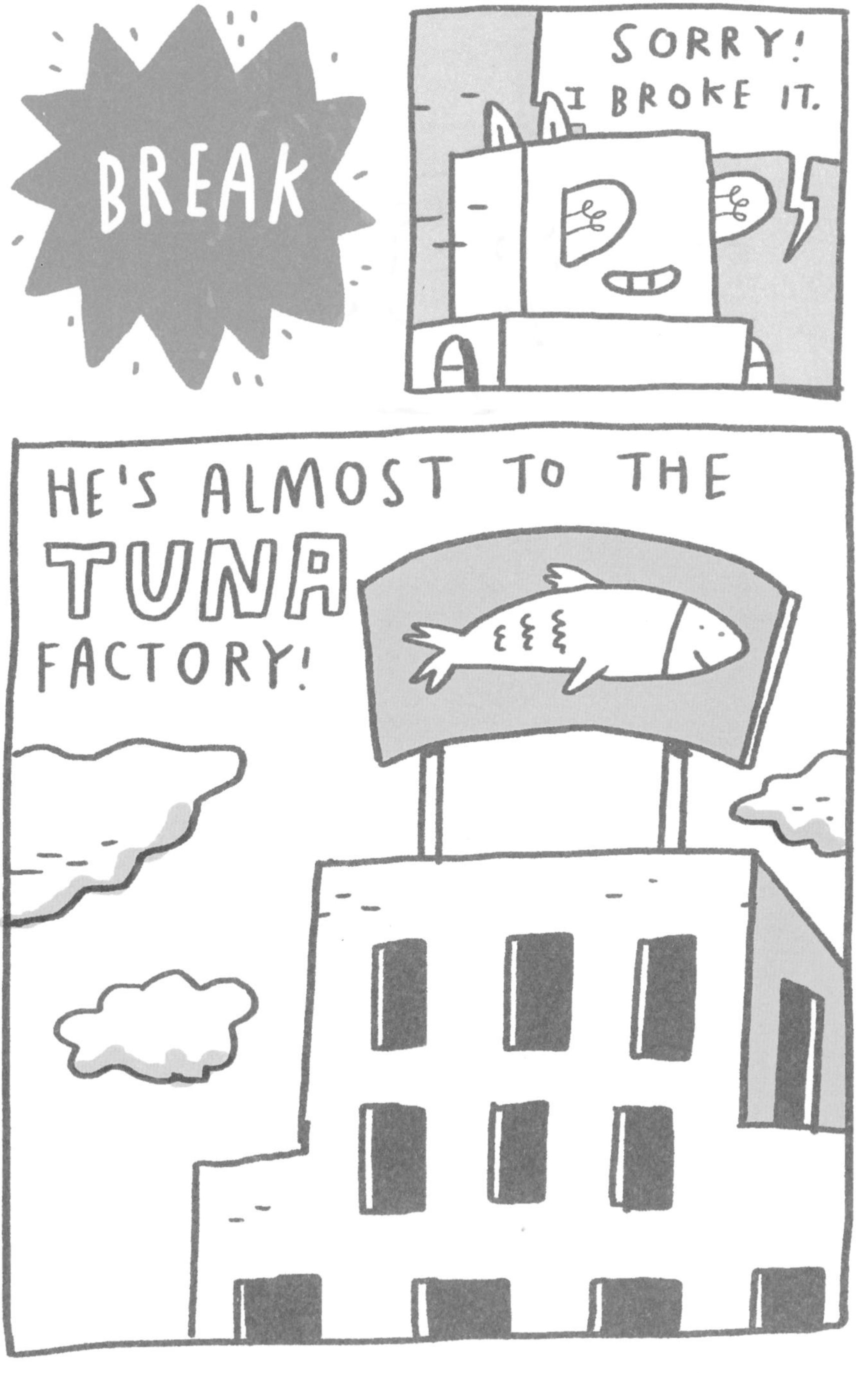
BREAK
SORRY! I BROKE IT.
HE'S ALMOST TO THE TUNA FACTORY!

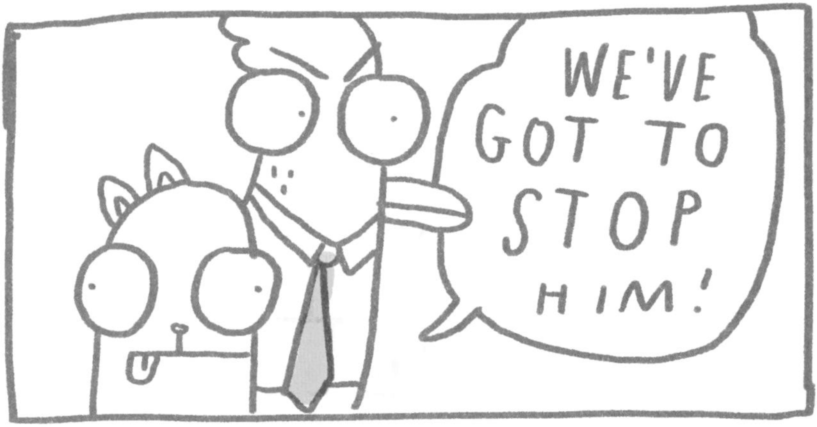
WE'VE GOT TO STOP HIM!

IT'S TIME FOR YOUR BIGGEST DRAWING CHALLENGE EVER!

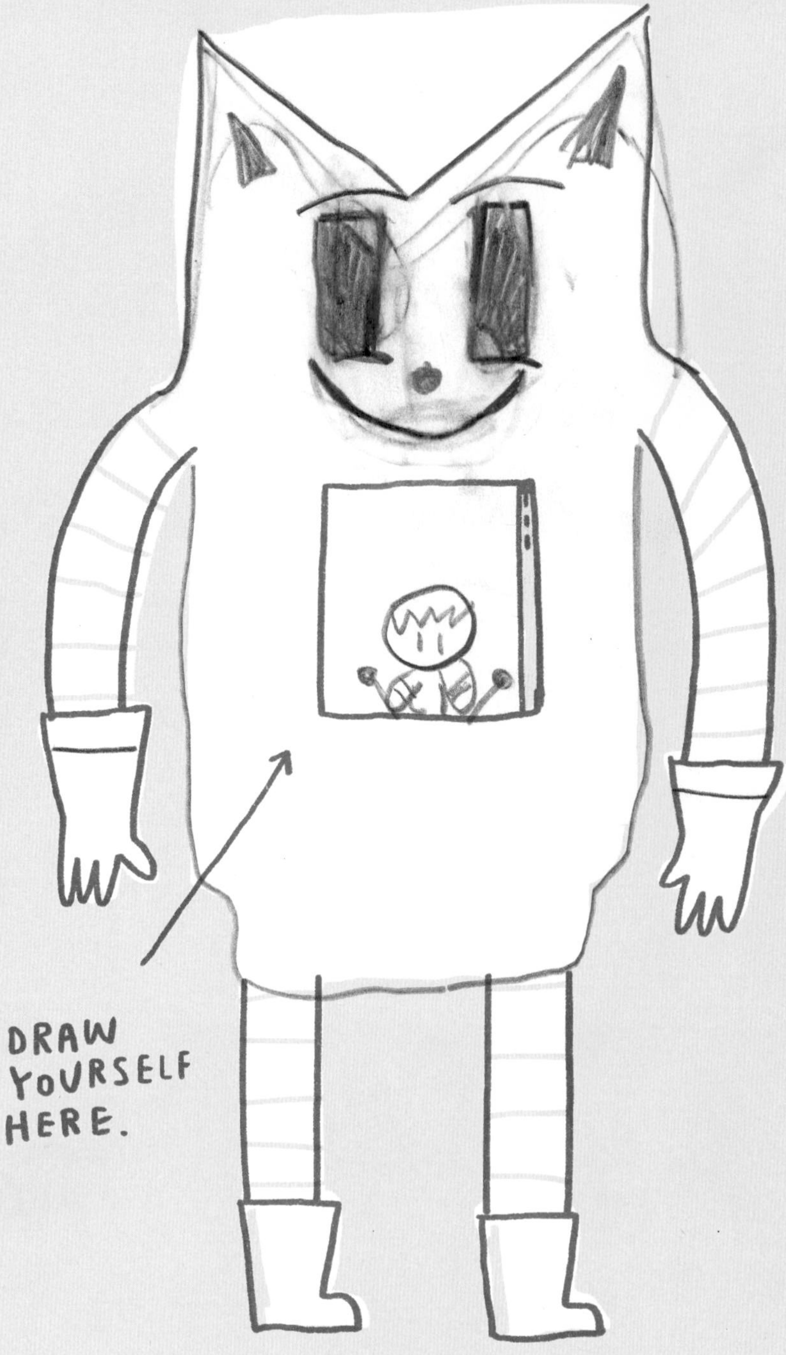
DRAW
YOURSELF
HERE.

DRAW THE ULTIMATE ROBO-ANIMAL TO STOP THE ROBO-CAT!

- WHAT KIND OF ANIMAL IS IT?

  Psunny *

- WHAT ARE ITS POWERS?

  eating lots of things

- WHAT DOES IT USE FOR FUEL?

  anything

- WHAT'S ITS WEAKNESS?

  eats to much things

* dog also Golden retriever

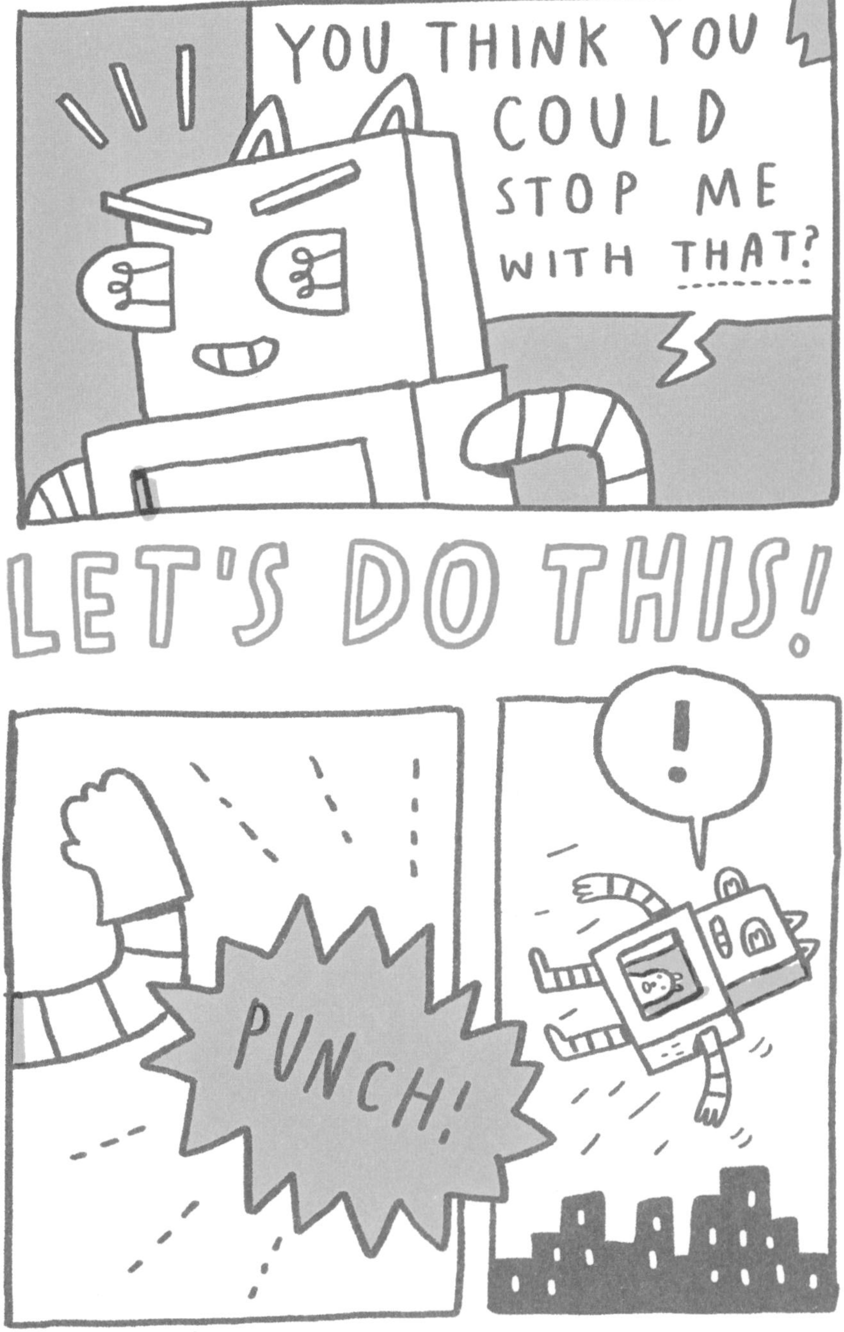
YOU THINK YOU COULD STOP ME WITH THAT?
LET'S DO THIS!
PUNCH!
!

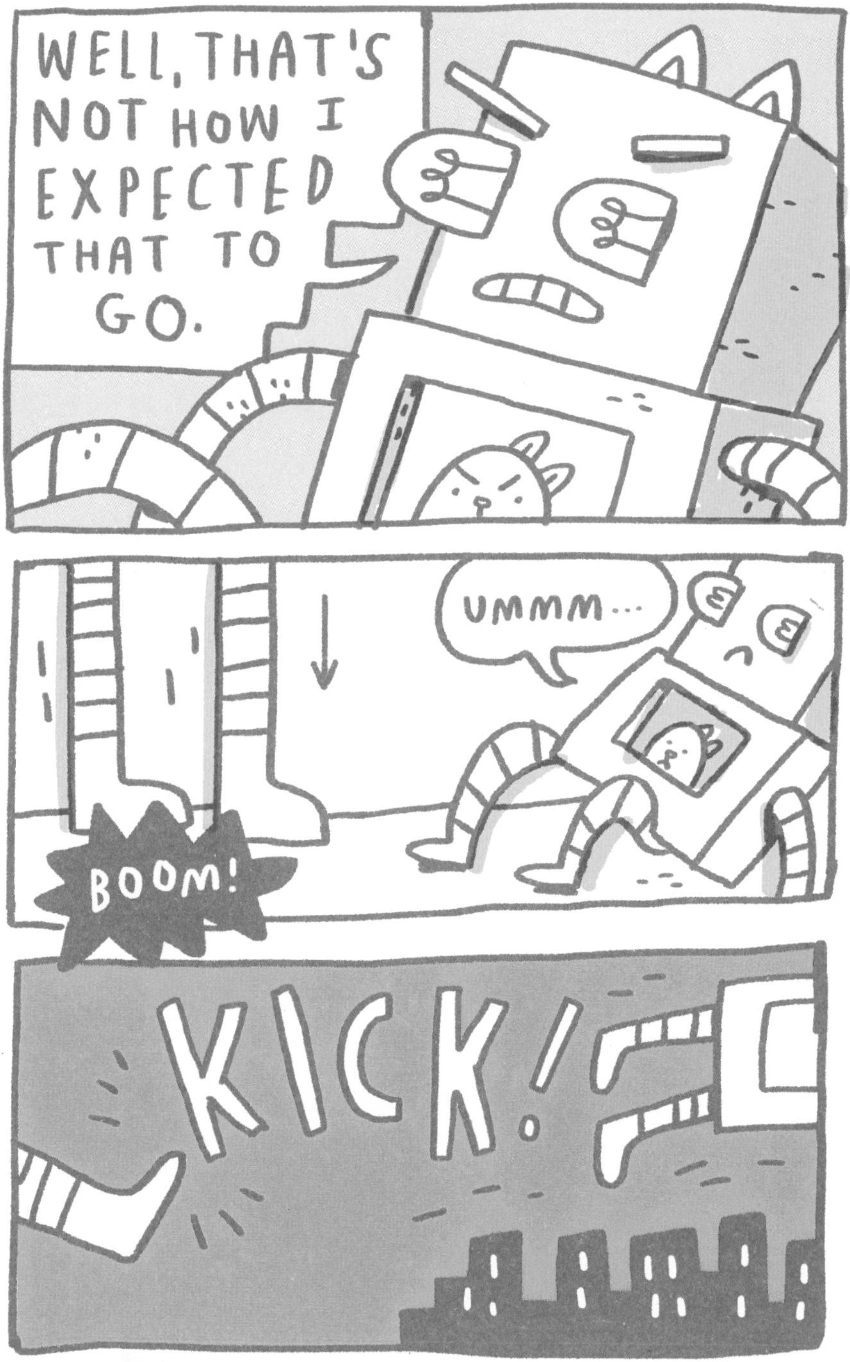
WELL, THAT'S NOT HOW I EXPECTED THAT TO GO.
UMMM...
BOOM!
KICK!

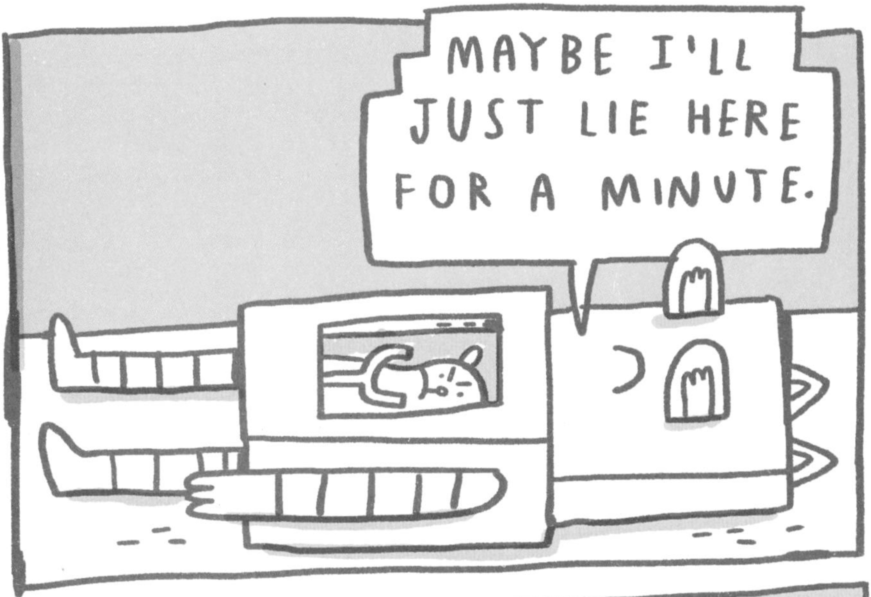
MAYBE I'LL JUST LIE HERE FOR A MINUTE.

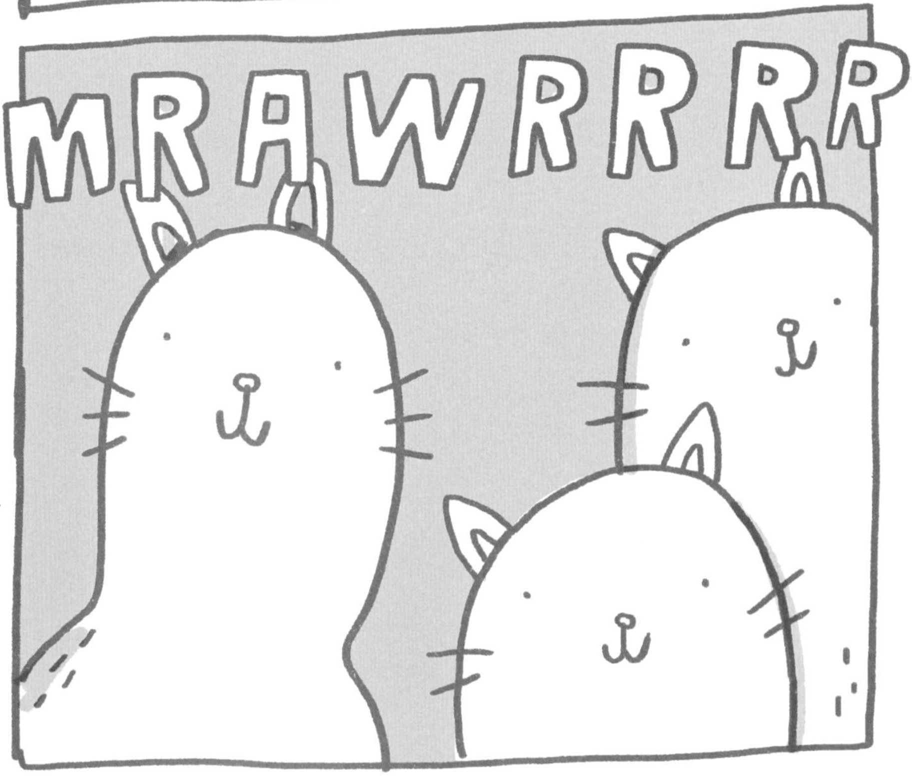
MRAWRRRR

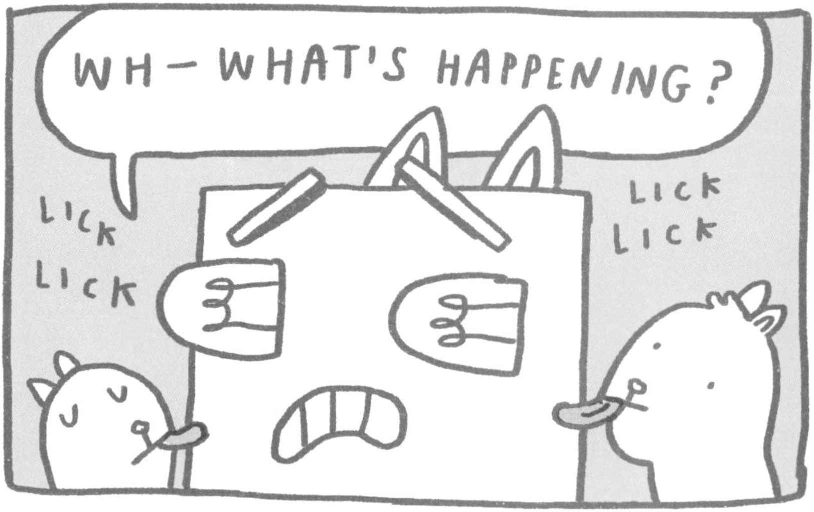
WH-WHAT'S HAPPENING?
LICK
LICK
LICK
LICK

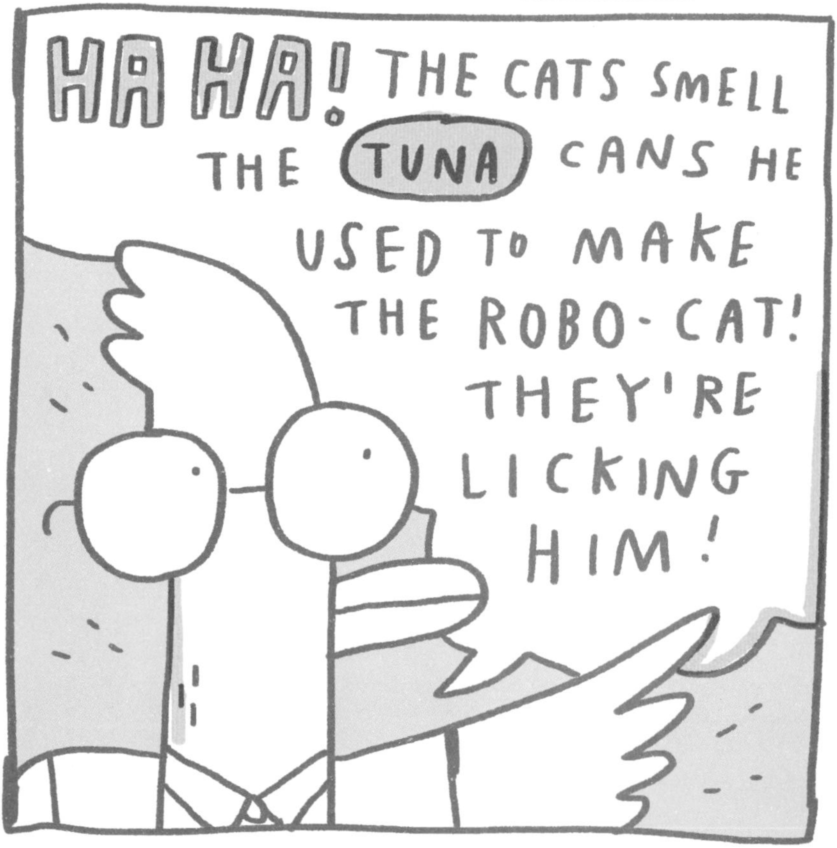
HA HA! THE CATS SMELL THE TUNA CANS HE USED TO MAKE THE ROBO-CAT! THEY'RE LICKING HIM!

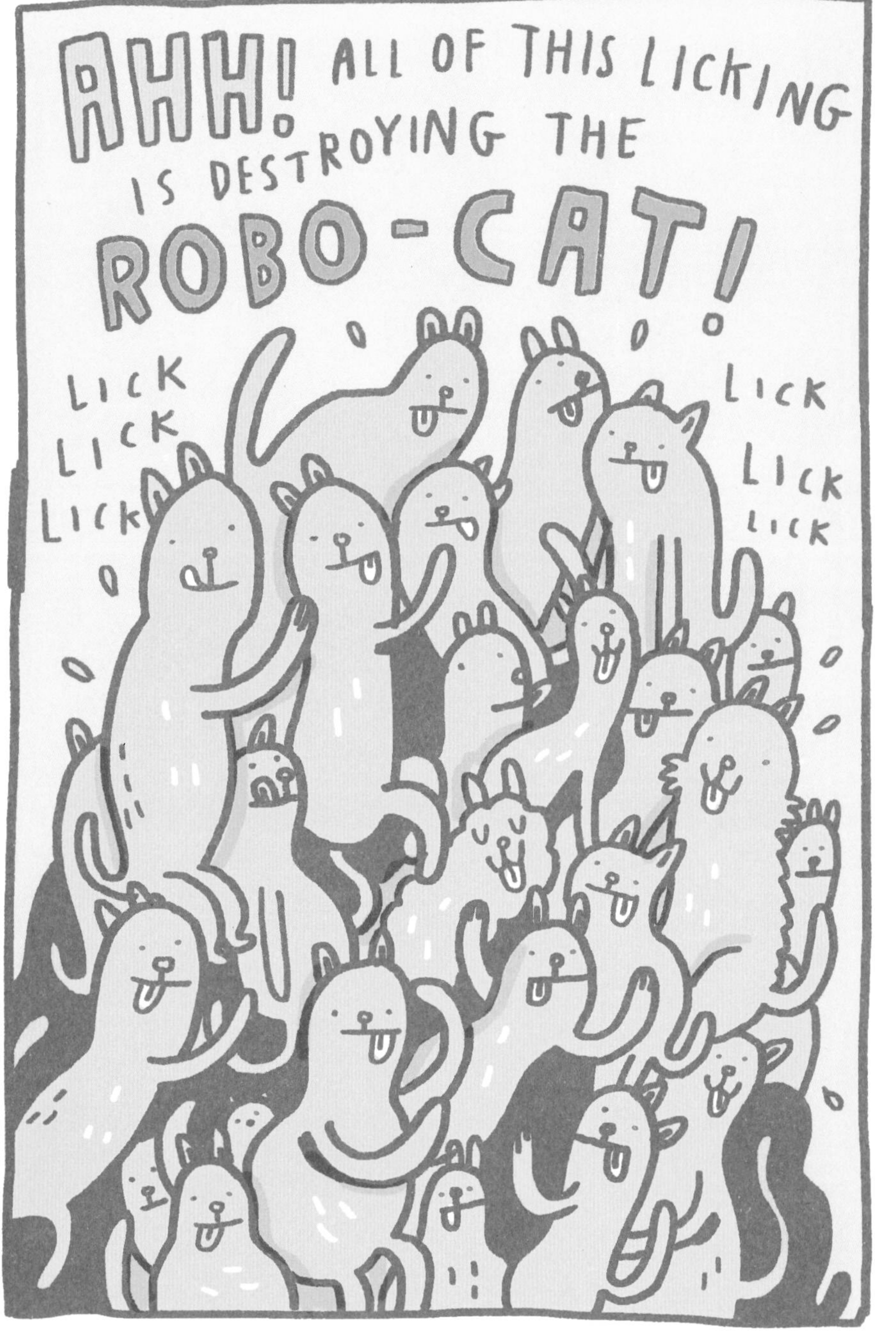
AHH! ALL OF THIS LICKING IS DESTROYING THE ROBO-CAT!
LICK
LICK
LICK
LICK
LICK
LICK

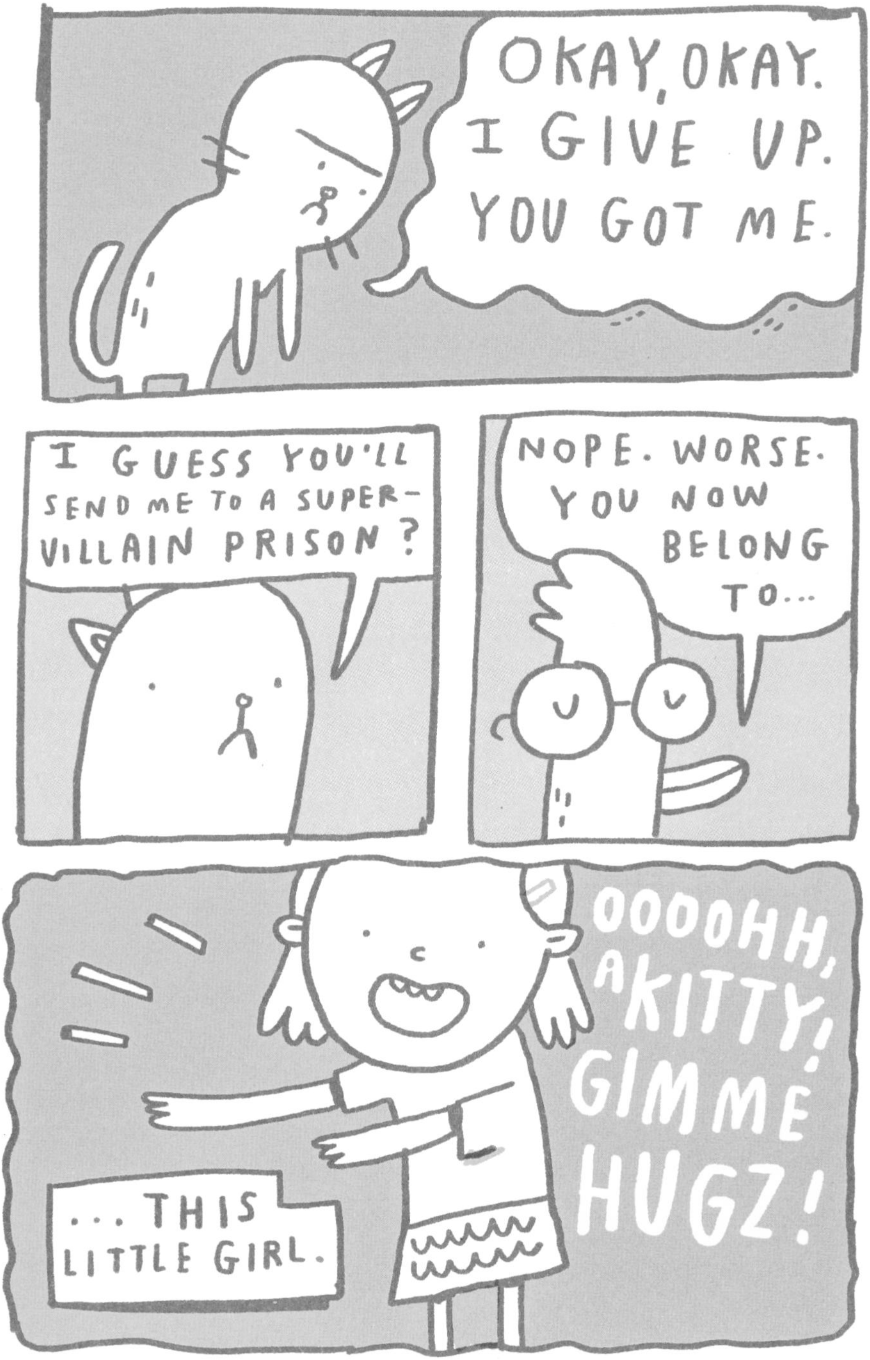
OKAY, OKAY. I GIVE UP. YOU GOT ME.
I GUESS YOU'LL SEND ME TO A SUPER-VILLAIN PRISON?
NOPE. WORSE. YOU NOW BELONG TO...
...THIS LITTLE GIRL.
OOOOHH, A KITTY! GIMME HUGZ!

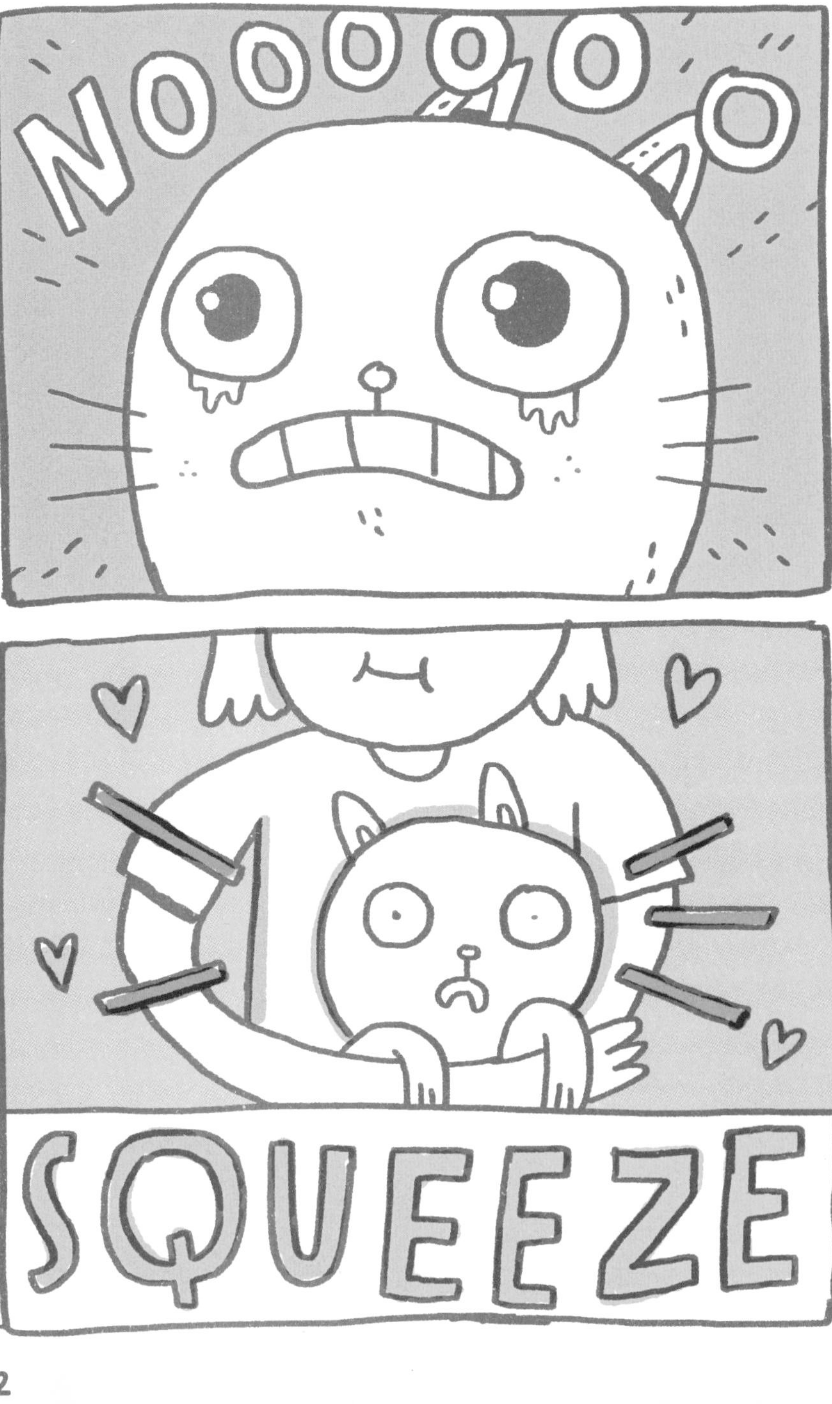
NOOOOOOOO
SQUEEZE

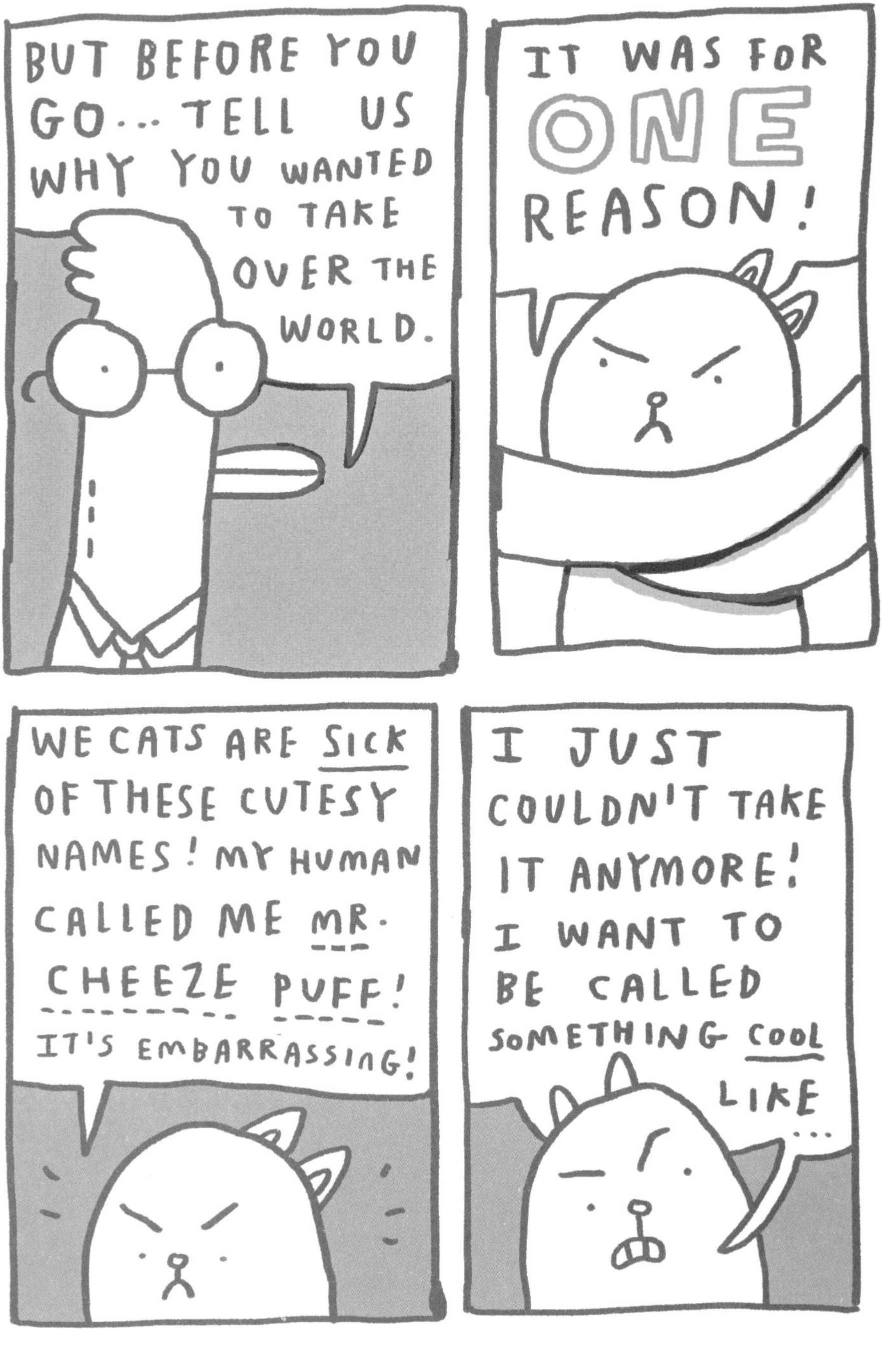
BUT BEFORE YOU GO... TELL US WHY YOU WANTED TO TAKE OVER THE WORLD.
IT WAS FOR ONE REASON!
WE CATS ARE SICK OF THESE CUTESY NAMES! MY HUMAN CALLED ME MR. CHEEZE PUFF! IT'S EMBARRASSING!
I JUST COULDN'T TAKE IT ANYMORE! I WANT TO BE CALLED SOMETHING COOL LIKE...

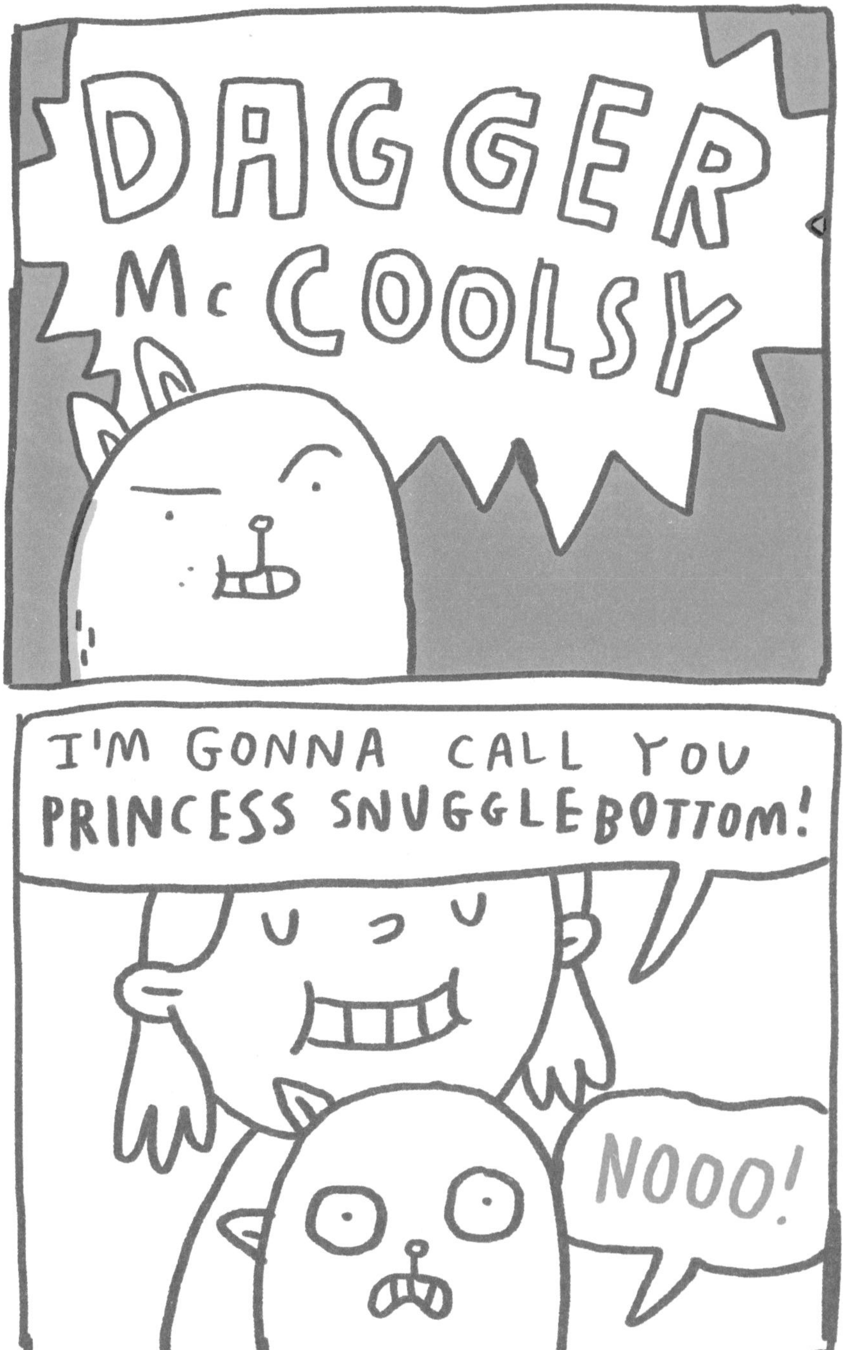
DAGGER McCOOLSY
I'M GONNA CALL YOU PRINCESS SNUGGLEBOTTOM!
NOOO!

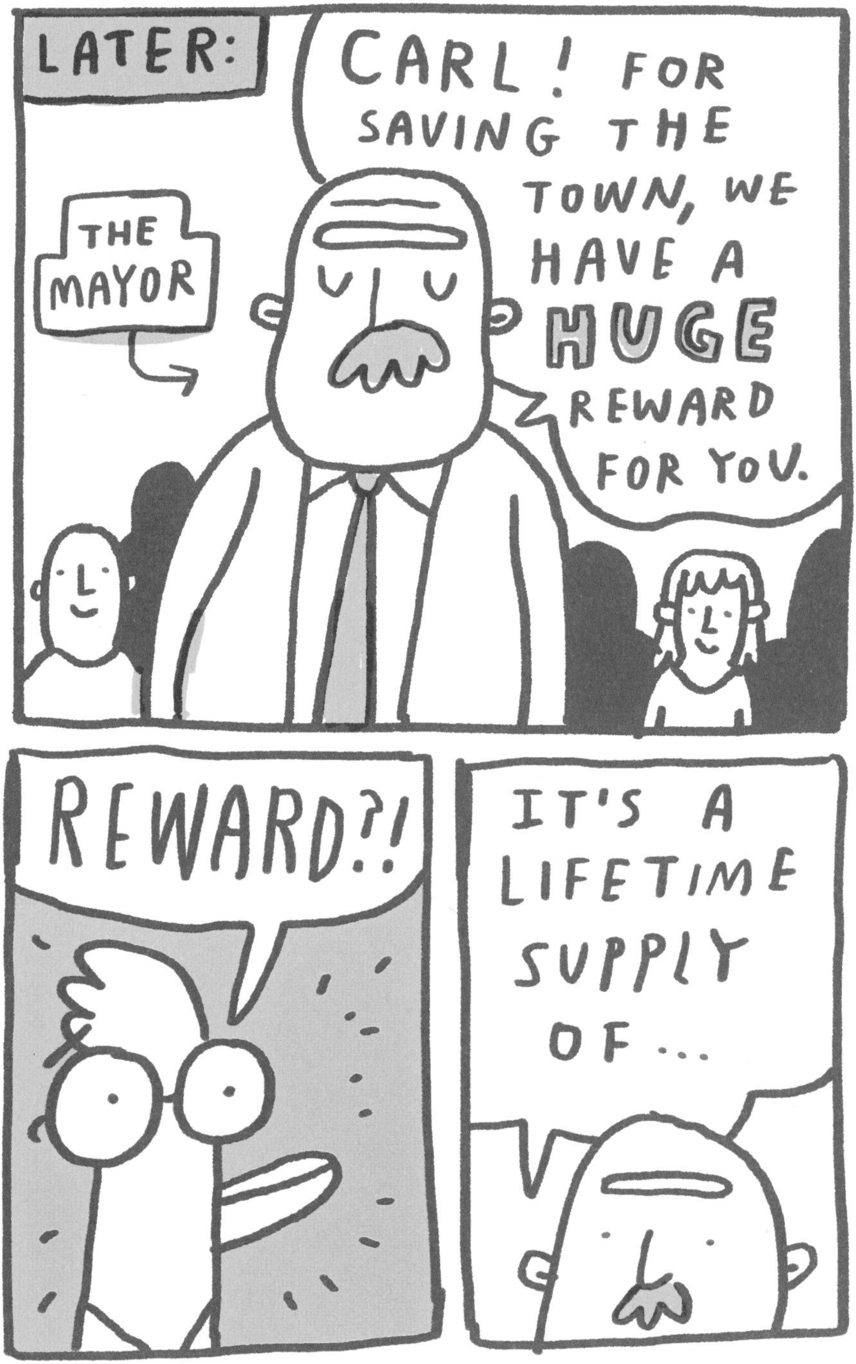
LATER:
CARL! FOR SAVING THE TOWN, WE HAVE A HUGE REWARD FOR YOU.
THE MAYOR
REWARD?!
IT'S A LIFETIME SUPPLY OF...

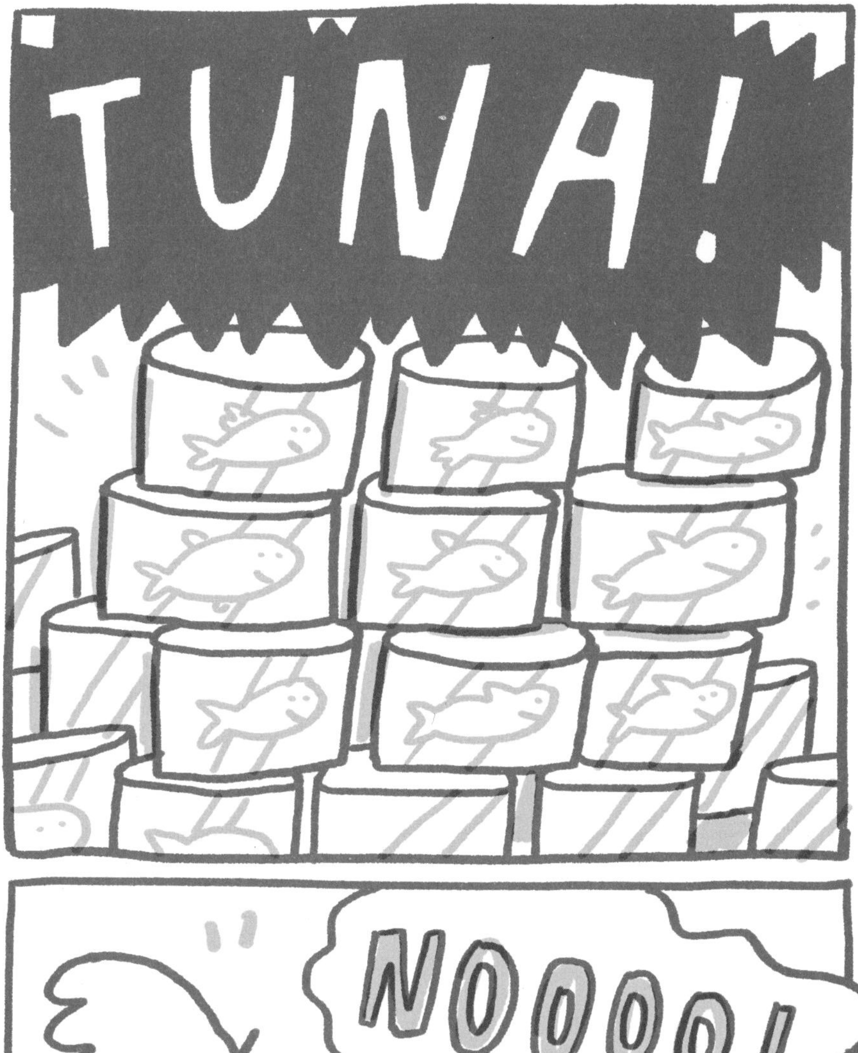
TUNA!

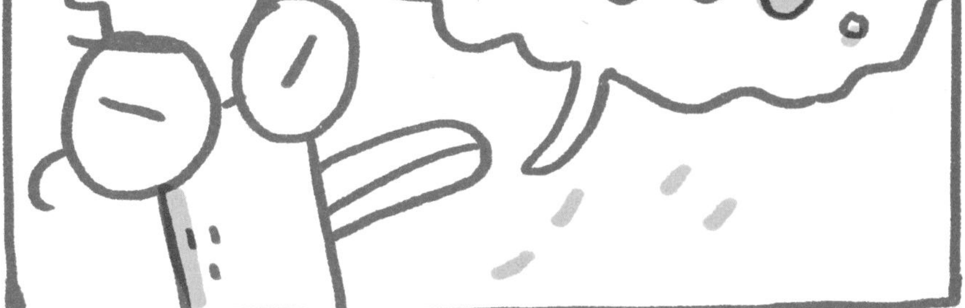
NOOOO!

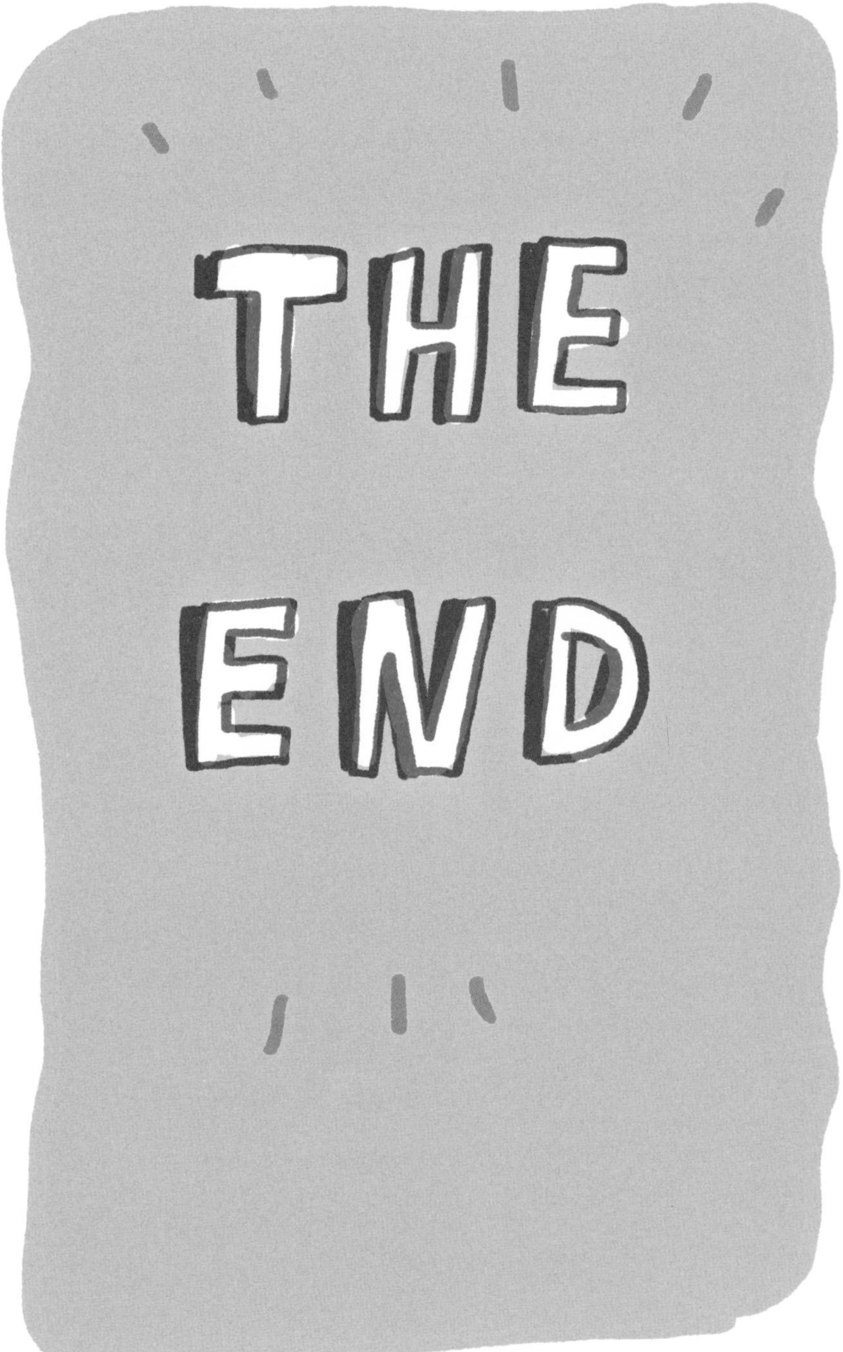
THE END

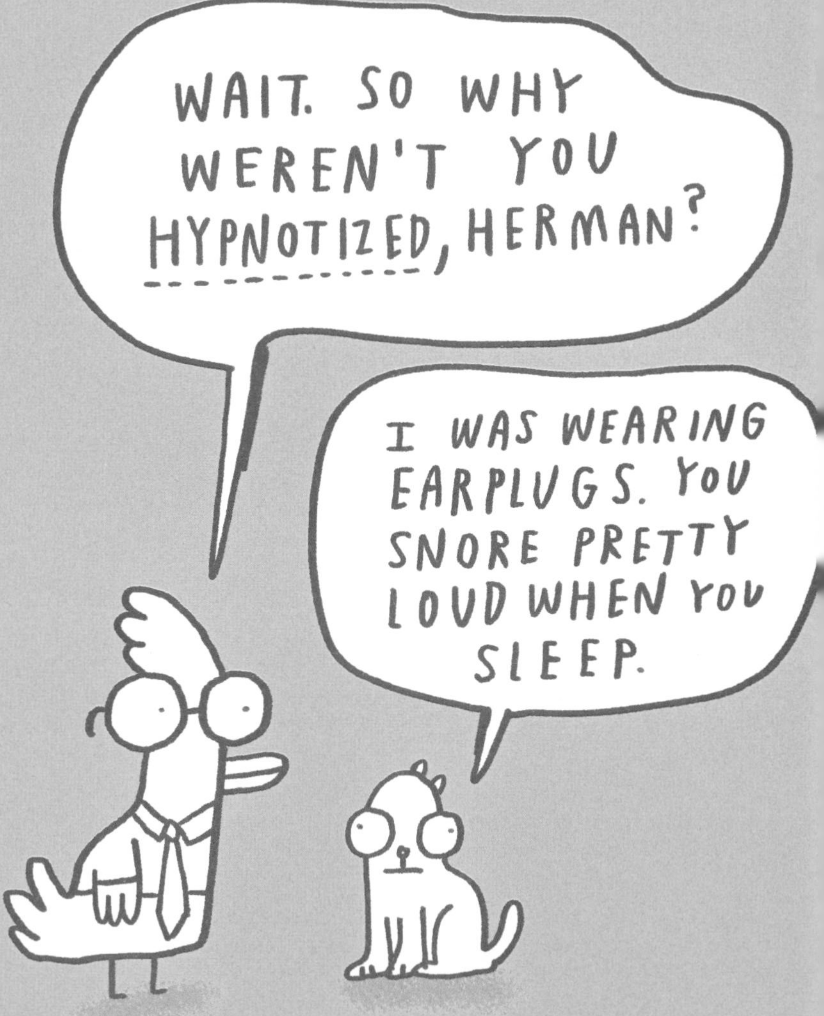

WAIT. SO WHY WEREN'T YOU HYPNOTIZED, HERMAN?
I WAS WEARING EARPLUGS. YOU SNORE PRETTY LOUD WHEN YOU SLEEP.

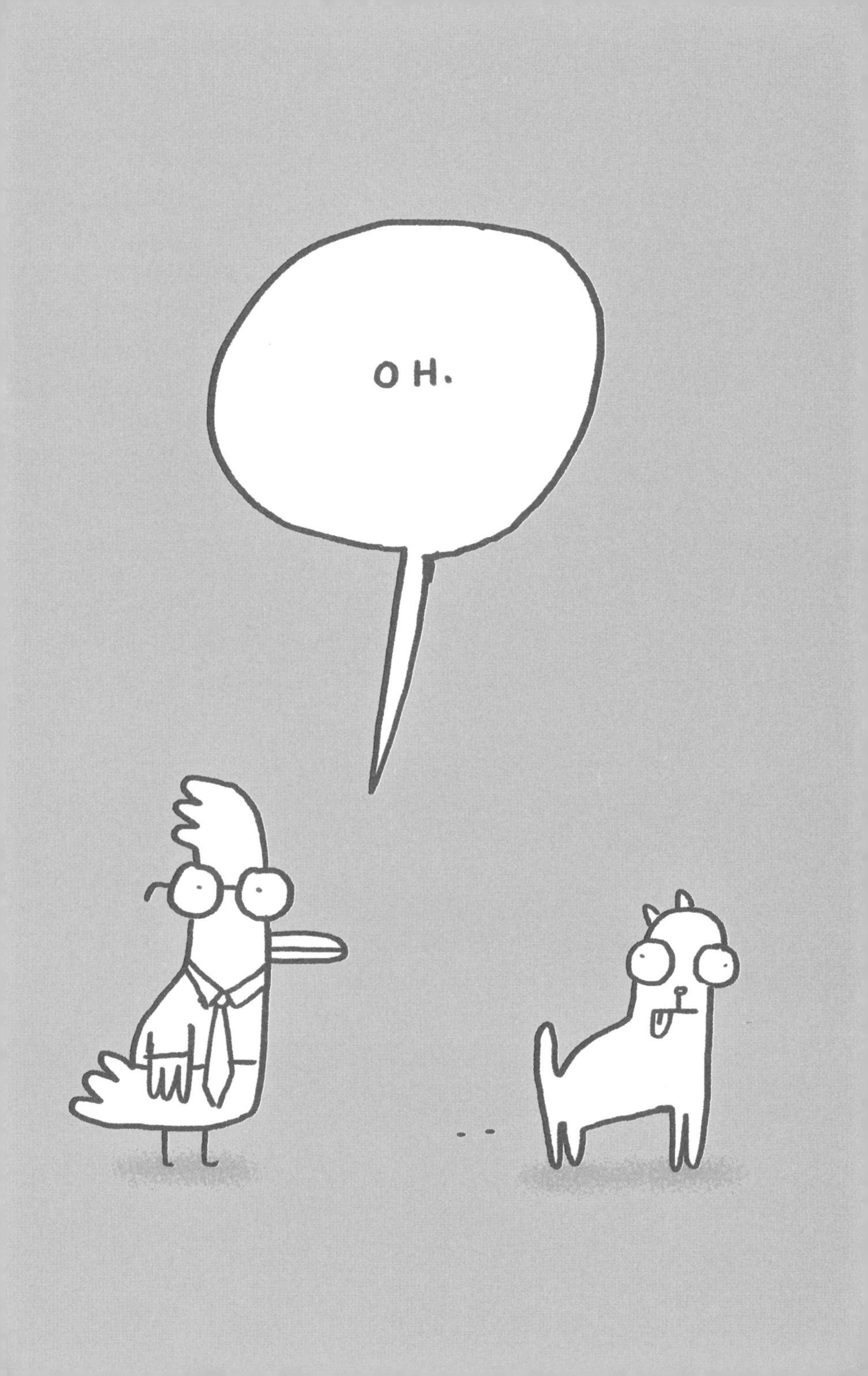
OH.

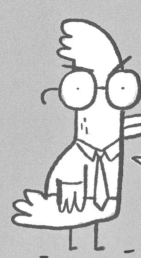

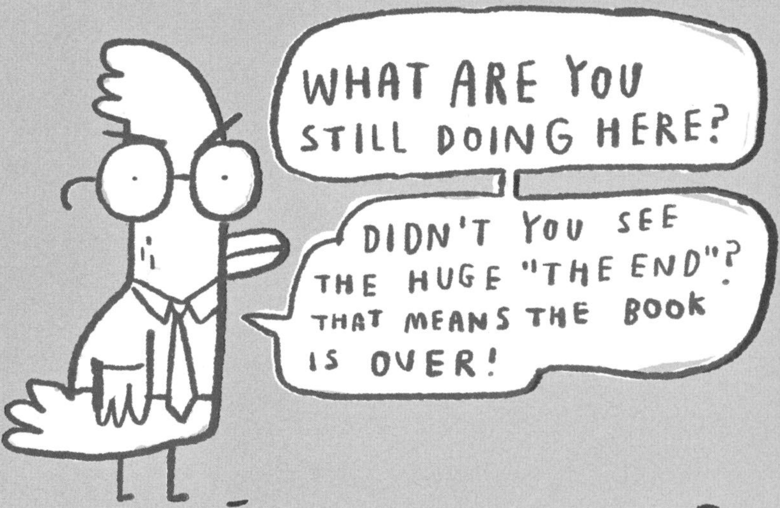

WHAT ARE YOU STILL DOING HERE?
DIDN'T YOU SEE THE HUGE "THE END"? THAT MEANS THE BOOK IS OVER!

READY FOR MORE DOODLE ADVENTURES?

CHECK OUT THE FIRST TWO ACTION-PACKED BOOKS IN THE SERIES

BOOK 1
DOODLE ADVENTURES
THE SEARCH FOR THE SLIMY SPACE SLUGS!
YOU DRAW THE STORY!
MIKE LOWERY
BOOK 2
DOODLE ADVENTURES
THE PURSUIT OF THE PESKY PIZZA PIRATE!
ARRR!
YOU DRAW THE STORY!
MIKE LOWERY

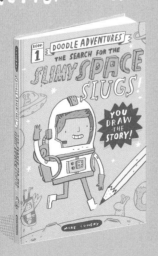

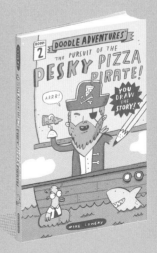

DID YOU DRAW IN YOUR BOOK?!

GREAT! SHOW IT OFF!

GET AN ADULT TO POST IT ON SOCIAL MEDIA WITH #DOODLEADVENTURES

OR MAYBE YOU'D PREFER TO DRAW CARL IN A FUNNY OUTFIT?

DON'T YOU DARE!

AND CHECK OUT MORE STUFF BY THE AUTHOR AT: MIKELOWERY.COM

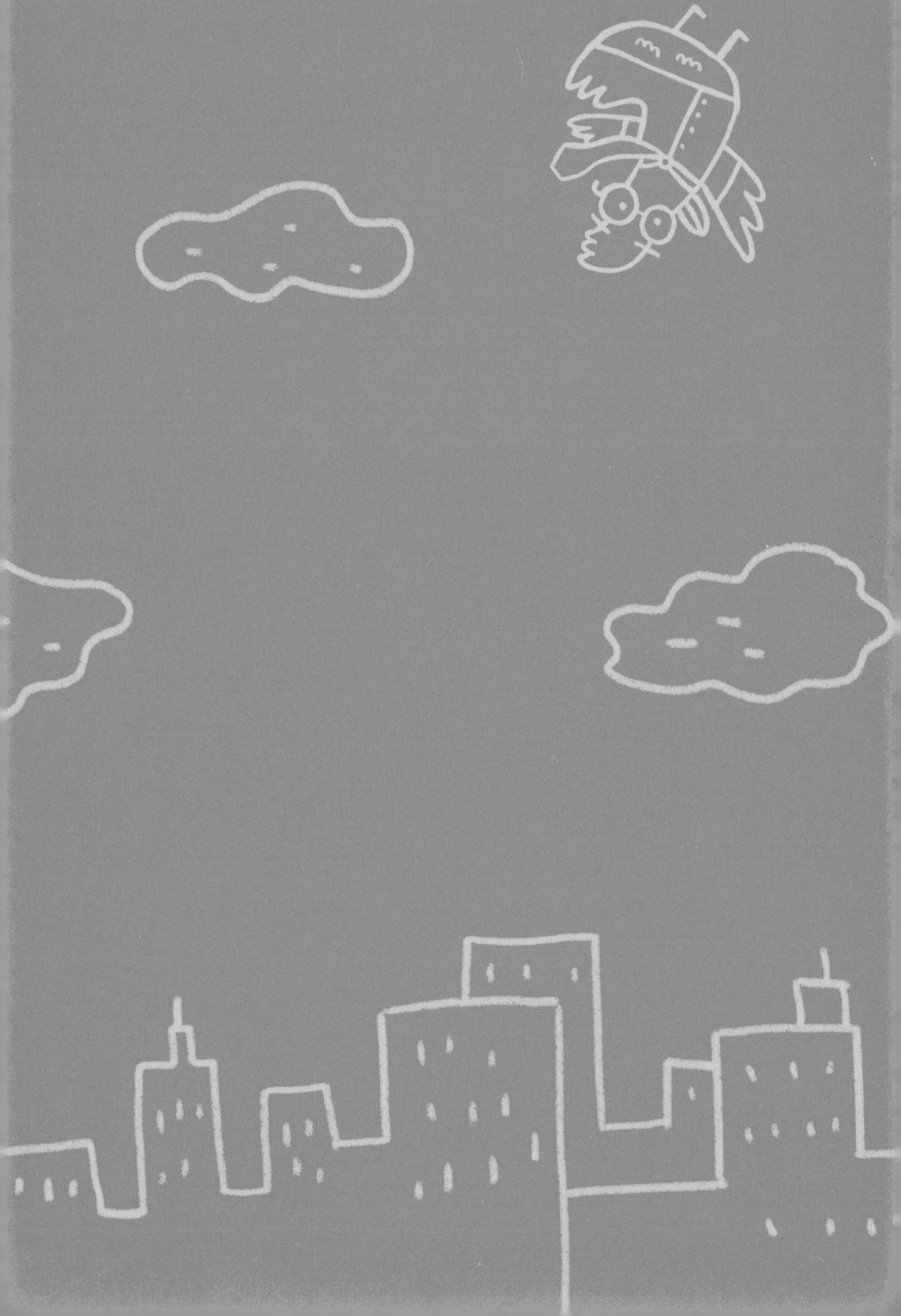

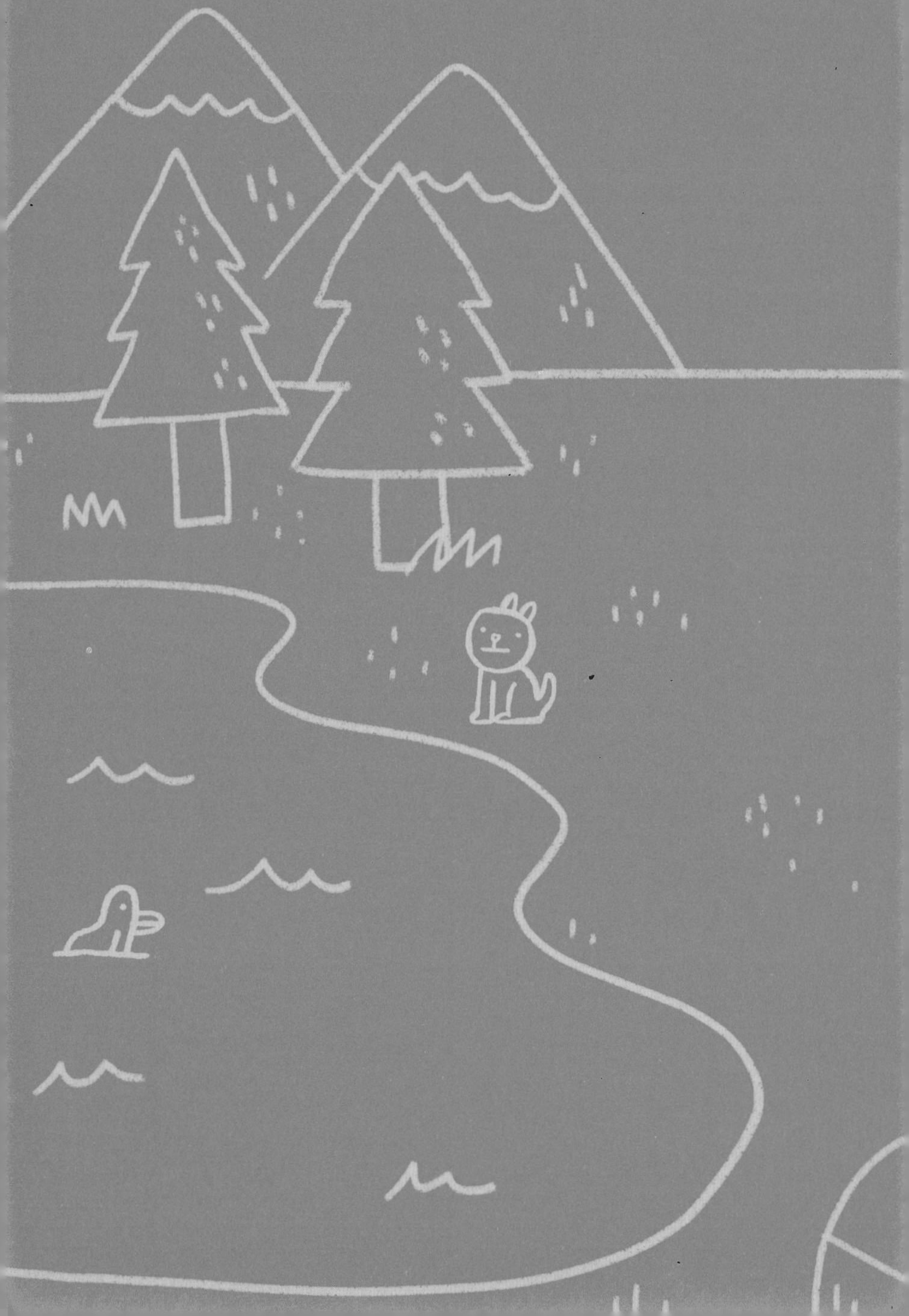